SUPERBAD

SUPERBAD
STORIES & PIECES

BEN GREENMAN

INTRODUCTION AND NOTES
BY LAURENCE ONGE

McSweeney's Books

McSWEENEY'S BOOKS
429 Seventh Avenue
Brooklyn, NY 11215

Cover painting by Mark Tansey

For more information about McSweeney's see www.mcsweeneys.net.
For more information about Ben Greenman, see www.bengreenman.com.

Published in the United States by McSweeney's Books
Portions of this work have previously appeared in The New Yorker,
The Mississippi Review Web Edition, and McSweeney's.

McSweeney's and colophon are registered trademarks
of McSweeney's, a privately held company with
wildly fluctuating resources.

First published in the United States by McSweeney's, 2001

Manufactured in Iceland by Oddi Printing

1   3   5   7   9   10   8   6   4   2

Library of Congress Cataloging-in-Publication Data
ISBN: 0-9703355-7-1

For my parents

SUPERBAD

CONTENTS

EDITOR'S INTRODUCTION

By *Laurence Onge*

Benjamin Greenman is not the first of my former students to embark upon a career in literature, nor will he be the last. In fact, just last week I was privileged to read a short story by a young man some ten years Mr. Greenman's junior who already has a rather impressive command of plot and character development. But if Mr. Greenman is not the first or the last of this species, he is the specimen closest to my heart. When he enrolled in my creative writing class some dozen summers ago, I had recently suffered from the first of what has been, to date, a troika of rather massive heart attacks. I was in the process of reassessing my life, and deciding that I should have made more stringent demands on those around me, that I should have raised my standards higher than they had been previously—although, I dare say, you are not likely to find many former students who would characterize me as a relativist or a democrat. At any rate, Mr. Greenman's class is a class I remember well, for I spent most of the session raging at them. I felt that they were hopeless, that they were charlatans and clowns, and I took every opportunity to tell them so. Of all the students in the class, there were only four or five who seemed to accept my criticism as fact rather than as dyspepsia, and even fewer than that who persisted with their writing despite my rather harsh words. Mr. Greenman was one of the persistent ones, and for that I am glad. His persistence seems to have served him well, and I have been pleased to help him select work for this collection.

With that said, I must confess that a bit of the judge still remains within me, and that I still believe that class, more than any other, to be composed of the most problematic writers I have ever taught. It is not that they were without talent, only that their talent seemed so rarely to manifest itself in the pieces that they wrote. Mr. Greenman was one of the strongest of the bunch, but I cannot tell you how many times over the years I have groaned audibly at one his pieces of writing, certain that it was doomed to a kind of aesthetic stillbirth. It is not, as I once explained to him, that he is not imaginative, but rather that his imagination is applied to grand ideas about his abilities rather than grand ideas he is able to articulate on the page. Younger colleagues of mine have suggested that the parodic japery of some of these shorter pieces is somehow illuminating the modern condition. I suppose they may be right, although I personally cannot see by this light.

Far more satisfying, to my tastes, are the musical interludes, which combine Mr. Greenman's light touch with his sense of the absurd and are delightful fun. You might not think that an old man who has had three heart attacks can recognize fun, but the truth is that I can recognize it more keenly than ever before: It is the only stop in the door of oncoming mortality. I cannot overpraise these musicals, so I will not even try: suffice it to say that they are, for me, like a light breeze of youth. My interest may also spring in part from my own involvement in their creation. Throughout the years, I have acted as a kind of *miglior fabbro* to Mr. Greenman, and I believe that I was responsible for his invention of the form. In a letter to Mr. Greenman, I once wrote, "Someone should pen satiric verse about the major figures of the day." Not six weeks later, a student of mine directed my attention to the first of these musicals. There are six of these musical interludes—I wish there were sixty.

I know, as few others know, how tirelessly Mr. Greenman has worked on this collection, and if diligence is a substitute for brilliance, then he is certainly one of the most brilliant young writers around. Still, I would be remiss in my duties as editor if I did not make my displeasure with some of these pieces known. For years, I have had a professional interest in the literatures of Italy and of Russia, above all other countries; one of the reasons I was interested in Mr. Greenman's work was that he shares the same tastes. Perhaps I read certain pieces overzealously; perhaps Mr. Greenman's fascination with those literary traditions produced in him a kind of paralysis. Whatever the case, I feel, and have always felt, deeply divided on the merits of the stories in this collection with Italian and Russian settings. After months of debate, I finally prevailed upon Mr. Greenman to allow me to pen brief introductions for these pieces—there are four of them—in the hopes of giving them a boost of sorts, and of preparing readers for the slight disappointment that they may, despite their generous natures, feel.

ILL IN '99

I was ill in '99. I got better from the turn of the century on—something about the weather, or my wife, or the hopeful way people looked at me in the street. But by 2011, I was dying again and there was nothing that anyone could do about it.

Sky hours measure how long you've been around. I remember them from my childhood. There were only sky hours then—sky hours in the crystal fifties, the brilliant sixties, the broad seventies. Stone hours measure how long you have left. After '99, I had mostly stone hours. I wasn't an old man when the illness first came on. I had some youth still. But I had less than I imagined.

I was sick at the same time as Merv Griffin, the famous talk-show host and game-show tycoon who was later elected to the U.S. Senate. Merv was much older than me, but some mornings I felt as old as Merv. This was a result of the illness, certainly, and by that I mean my illness and not Merv's. Merv had cancer, which eats you slowly. I had something much hungrier.

In the restless nineties I worked in construction, a real muscle-man profession. I carried iron beams from place to place, lugged bales of welding wire, fastened flat countersunk head rivets. Some days I worked without a hard hat. That's how tough a customer I was. By 2005, I was long off the sites, bumped up to the executive tier, so it only made sense for me to quit the construction racket and move on to be the nation's Secretary of Publicity. I headed up The Department of How Things Are, which was located in a menacing ash-black building right across the street from the petite, pink offices of The Department of How Things Should Be. My job mostly involved circling pictures of women's breasts in fashion magazines. It wasn't the easiest job in the world—I had to use one of those permanent markers, and the squeaking and the smell damned near drove me nuts some days—but I got really good at it, and by my third month there I rarely accidentally circled the head or the hand.

Castelloni and Davies were my right-hand men.

Castelloni was an actor. When I was a kid he was the star of a TV show called "Russell Aikens," as Russell Aikens, who was a kind of superhero. His slogan was "Geography Teacher by Day, Crimefighter by Night." That slogan became a euphemism for gay people and the double life they led. If my friends and I saw a particularly swishy guy out on the street, we'd elbow one another in the chest. "Geography teacher by day, crimefighter by night," we'd snicker, and eventually we just shortened it to "geography teacher by day." Castelloni wasn't gay. He was a mean bastard who was closer in character to the assassins and mob bosses he went on to play in the movies. He would call you what he wanted to call you and hit you when you were down. Once we were debating how to tell the nation about drilling on Utah's Kaiparowits Plateau. "We should just tell them," Castelloni said. His thick face was a terrible red. "Tell them where we're going to drill, and if they don't like it, we'll just drill a hole into their fucking skulls with one of those cordless drills! If we can't do the job, maybe we should farm it out to those pansy-ass pinheads at the Department of How Things Should Be." At the end of his rather persuasive speech, he was screaming so loud that he clutched his jaw as if he had dislocated it.

Davies was a geography teacher by day.

We worked as a crack team, the three of us. Or rather, they worked and I supervised. The breast-circling kept me busy most of the day, and at night I would go home and eat a simple meal off of one of the commemorative plates my ex-wife and I had collected—the Space Shuttle plate, the Berlin Wall dismantling plate, or the Canadian Unpleasantness plate. Then I'd watch some TV, go to sleep, and wake up early enough to be back in the office by 8 a.m. As a result, I only had a few minutes each day to design the nation's intellectual and moral agenda and write up press releases that would advance that agenda. But what a glorious few minutes! One day I wrote this release, which went out along the wires in time to make the evening news:

Our Good Citizens: Great leaders from our past, like Roosevelt, Wilson, and Johnson, rose to the tops of nations that required their leadership. But the Americas of Roosevelt, Wilson, and Johnson no longer exist; they are not the America we see today. Roosevelt, Wilson and Johnson spent their lives wrestling with issues vital to the nation's survival—with industrialization, with aggression from overseas, with an internal inequity that threatened to erupt into a sort of cultural civil war. Today these are not concerns. The problems of our time are more difficult. They are not about technological progress. We have more technological progress than we know how to handle. They are not about peacetime and wartime. The difference between those two states disappeared a long time ago. They are not about race. All races are equalized, if not always equal. Now, as we look toward the middle of this new century, we must disenthrall ourselves with the concerns of the past and confront the issues of the present, which will become the issues of the future. I will now list those issues. Goodbye, and goodnight.

It was a version of a speech by John Kennedy, right down to the word "disenthrall," but with one important difference. My release had no point. I had the buildup in place. I had all of America waiting for the issues. But then—no bang. No pitch. No nothing.

This was part of the plan.

In the time before the establishment of the Department, the entire nation—the men in suits, the women in skirts, the children who attested to the willingness of those men and women to couple with one another, if not always to connect—watched the goverrnment with an indifference that canted more toward contempt than resentment. They felt superior to their caretakers, above those who labored to give them a better life. They weren't afraid of government. They simply felt that it didn't serve their needs. This was shortly after the nineties drew to a close. As a result of this contempt of government, many television and film celebrities from the broad seventies were elected to government—not just Merv Griffin, who to date has served four terms in the U.S. Senate, but Representatives Clint Eastwood, Dustin Hoffman, Mike Douglas, and Faye Dunaway. Contrary to the myth perpetuated by some of our less reputable historians, popular movie star Robert Redford did not pursue a career in politics, although there was a one-term Representative from Utah named Robert Redfern who was also a Kleagle in the Salt Lake City Ku Klux Klan. At any rate, the formation of the Department of How Things Are galvanized the public, satisfying the clumsy, childlike need to be organized that had gone unaddressed during the broad seventies, the booming eighties, and the restless nineties. In its early years, the Department offered a sanctuary from the terrors of a chaotic world, sending out recommendation memos that instructed "Our Good Citizens" (for this was how we addressed them, always, as a form of positive reinforcement) what they should watch on television, which magazines they should read, in what order they should go through the sections of the morning newspaper (sports first, then news, then business news, then entertainment). Department officials encouraged people to turn in their neighbors when they discovered them violating the recommendations.

In the second half-decade of operation, though, the

Department's philosophy shifted. I was primarily responsible for the shift, having arrived from the world of construction with a bee in my bonnet about reforming the government's propaganda operation. The first weekend of my administration, I scheduled a retreat with my top managers—Castelloni, Davies, and a third man who had the strange name of Weaver Cinnamon. Weaver Cinnamon was the youngest of us all, no more than thirty when he joined the Department in 2005. He was from a tiny Arkansas town named Subiaco, where the Cinammon family owned a neighborhood grocery. He had risen through the ranks quickly, in part because he was a quick study, in part because he had a good personality, and in part because he was the most handsome man anyone had ever seen, with a strong jawline, steel-gray eyes, and perfect, rugged features that looked as if they had been sculpted with God's own chisel. Weaver Cinnamon was hard to look at, he was so handsome, but he was easy to promote.

We took our retreat on the Northeast coast of Canada, which was still a friendly nation then, and on the second afternoon there Weaver Cinnamon went hiking by himself. He made it all the way up a small mountain near the camp, arriving just at sunset, and then stood there, silhouetted by the red sky, the shelf of the ridge jutting out beneath him. Off in the distance, a sailboat was in irons in the water, and from where we stood, on the lower plateau, it looked as if the sailors, too, were watching Weaver Cinnamon as he stood atop the ridge. "Isn't he beautiful?" asked Davies.

"Shut up!" snapped Castelloni, but without his usual ire. Even Castelloni liked Weaver Cinammon.

The next morning, after listening to a radio address by Senator Griffin that condemned a recent string of church burnings in the New Southwest—Merv was still going strong then, not yet cancer-ridden—I called the group together, only to find that Weaver Cinnamon was nowhere to be found. Neither Castelloni nor Davies had seen him since we had all seen him standing on the mountain. We knew better than to mess with the Canadian wild ourselves, so we called the Mounties quickly, and in about ten hours, they brought back the chewed corpse of Weaver Cinnamon. "Killer wolves," the Mountie captain said. "Maybe bears." He wasn't so bad-looking himself, this Mountie captain, but he was nothing like Weaver Cinnamon. We buried Cinnamon the next day in a small cemetery whose other residents seemed to be members of the same family, and the day after that, back in Washington, my two top lieutenants and I, all three of us still tearful from the loss of our youngest and handsomest colleague, sat down to map out our plan for the Department. That's how we came to be the most powerful part of the government—more powerful than the Department of the Interior, more powerful than the Department of Defense, more powerful than the Fed or the President. We were impelled forward by grief.

The decade dragged on. We dodged boredom. I can't go into the details of our activities—they are all classified—but suffice it to say that we destroyed a few major religions, commissioned the occasional assassination, and circled more than two hundred thousand pairs of breasts between January 1, 2006 and December 1, 2010. The figures for this year haven't yet been tabulated. We also released a steady stream of speeches and statements that kept America numb and kept Americans guessing. What was the government thinking? What was the government doing? We weren't telling. Then last Wednesday, Castelloni came up to me. He was screaming, as always. "Moron!" he said. "Go to the doctor! Idiot!" The advice came out of nowhere—since '99, I had been the picture of health, with only an occasional onset of flu-like symptoms or floaters in my field of vision I attributed to too much television. Other than that, I hadn't had so much as a nosebleed. But if Castelloni noticed something, I was willing to consider the possibility. He was always a very perceptive man. Davies visited me in my office later, and sat on my desk and nervously pinched the pleats of his pants. "Chief," he said, "you seem awful. Your circles around these breasts are irregularly shaped, and sometimes you're X'ing them instead of circling them. Plus, you look haggard and drawn, and at least twenty years older than you are." Then he started telling me about how his new lover's parents hadn't really accepted him yet. I went down to give some blood, in part so that the doctors could determine how sick I was and in part to escape Davies's endless confession. He did that kind of thing—oh they won't accept me, oh my life's so hard—about twice a week. It got old fast. The med staff made me wait for about an hour, and then the nurse ushered me in. She was tall, and had reddish hair, and she kept palpating my stomach and asking me how it felt.

While I waited for the results of my tests, I told the nurse about how just days before, I had convinced a libertarian governor of a traditionally Republican state to sign a bill that required criminals convicted of multiple crimes to be sentenced under whichever offense carried the highest penalty. The nurse was impressed. She was a politics buff, she said, and had always had difficulty finding other people to talk to about the pressing issues of our time.

"I can imagine," I said. What I didn't say is that not only could I imagine the nation's apathy, but that I had induced the nation's apathy. It was part of the plan. Each day, Castelloni, Davies, and I set out to strip Americans of what little of their political interest remained. That was why we released so many confusing and nonsensical statements. And we had, for the most part, succeeded. Still fawning over me—I guess it's not every day that the Secretary of Publicity drops by for a checkup—the nurse asked me out for a drink, and off we went. The two of us got really sloshed on boilermakers, and before I knew it she was talking about Jimmy Carter, who was President at the end of the broad seventies. "He was such a good man," she said, "and so maligned for no good reason."

"I don't know," I said. "I'm somewhat partial to Ted Kennedy."

She wrinkled up her nose. "I just know him because he ran against Carter in the 1980 primaries." she said. "Wasn't he a drunk?"

"Probably," I said. "His wife Joan was. And Ted had his problems with the bottle, too, not to mention some difficulty with fidelity. I didn't see it, you know. I heard things. But despite those flaws, he was a great leader. He lived through the assassinations of both his brothers—John, who was President in the brilliant sixties, and Robert, who ran for President. And he kept his influence in the Senate right through to his death."

"But Carter," she said, "restored morality to the nation. And despite soaring energy costs and a really problematic economy, not to mention tensions in the Middle East, he stabilized the country. Plus, after his Presidency, he kept helping people. I think he's one of the most important figures of the last forty years. He's right up there with Mike Douglas."

"Look," I said, "this is a silly conversation. Both Carter and Kennedy are long gone. What are we fighting about here? And why would you even mention someone like Mike Douglas? Douglas isn't even as important as Dick Cavett, and neither of them can really compare with Merv Griffin. Who negotiated a disengagement agreement with Honduras and Mexico? Who pushed through funding for the first residential space station? Who co-authored the Griffin-Jarvis Bill, which regulated privatized education? I mean, Griffin gets cancer, and still he's volunteering for more committee assignments."

"Well," she said, and then she said "well" again. She sounded angry. "By the way, I got your test results. You're dying."

"Hey," I said, somewhat taken aback. "If you don't want to talk about politics, that's fine with me. We could talk about movies."

"No," she said. "You're really dying. It might take a week, maybe a month. But you're about to be dead."

When I got home that night I collapsed on the couch and thought about death. I thought about Weaver Cinnamon, and how ugly and diminished his beautiful face had looked half-eaten by wolves, or bears, or whatever they were. Then I went to the digital phone book and tried in vain to find my ex-wife's number. Her name was Lisa and she was an American Indian. Lisa isn't a name often associated with American Indians, but Lisa looked like Cher, who was a famous singer at around the same time Merv Griffin was a famous talk-show host, and was also the co-host of her very own variety show, along with her husband Sonny Bono, a short singer who was later in government, though not with a position as important as mine or Merv Griffin's.

Lisa taught me many things about the spirit. That's the wonderful thing about American Indians. They are people of the spirit. They trap rabbits with their bare hands and use every part of the animal—the meat, the pelt, the teeth. They extract the rabbit's eyes and use them for native medicine, and the myelin that coats the rabbit's muscles is chemically altered in their factories and resold as a powerful industrial lubricant. But what they do to rabbits is only the beginning. These people build a bridge between the vast plains and the vast sky. In their mind, I mean. A bridge in their mind. With the materials of their spirits.

Lisa's hair was jet-black, much darker than mine. One night in '99, in the time of my first illness, my hair turned white. Snow-white, to be precise. And it did actually happen overnight. I went to bed with my hair as brown as shoe-leather, and woke with it as white as snow. I'm not sure how this happened, but it parallels the case of Bob Barker, who was a game-show host at the same time that Senator Merv Griffin had his talk show and Cher had her variety show. Those were the broad seventies, which represented the peak of talk shows until the restless nineties. In the nineties, even Clifton Chenier, who was an accordion player who specialized in a New Orleans music called zydeco, had his own morning talk show. In fact, Lisa was watching *Bonjour Chenier* the morning I woke up with my snow-white hair.

That was in '99, and we were young marrieds in the tender zone of early bliss. That's when we started to collect the commemorative plates. We collected the plates as if our love would last forever. It lasted somewhat less than forever—six years to be exact—and when it ended, Lisa smashed up the plate that depicted the public funeral of Don Henley, who was a popular singer before he was elected Governor of California and then martyred by an assassin's bullet. Then it was ought-eleven, and I was moving like a melody toward my final reward, and that's when I decided to call Lisa and set things right with her once and for all. The only problem was, I didn't know where to find her. Lisa had been a waitress and a bartender when she was my wife. When we split up, she went to work in a figurine factory. She was doing her part to help along the American Manufacturing Renaissance. She was gluing the huge plastic heads onto the tiny plastic bodies of Nancy Reagan dolls.

Soon after I learned I would die, I remembered what Lisa taught me about sky hours and stone hours. And soon after that, I went by the bar where she used to work and slapped the backs of the drunks who introduced us, who saw that we would be perfect for one another and build a house of perfect love in the sky. Tom Lehman was the oldest drunk there, about the same age as Senator Eastwood, and he was also one of my oldest friends. "Come outside with me, Tom," I said.

Outside, Tom and I sat on a bench. We talked about his ex-wife, and his kids, and his ailing mother, and then we talked about the recent wave of nostalgia for the broad seventies. "That Merv Griffin," said Tom Lehman, "do you think he is a geography teacher by day?"

"Maybe," I said. "But he's a great man, Tom." There was a lump in my throat. I couldn't help it. Thinking about Merv always got me choked up that way.

We talked more about the movies, and sports, and work. "How's the tit-circling biz?" Tom asked. I said it was fine. I asked Tom if he had heard from Lisa. Tom looked at me long and hard. "You don't know?"

"I guess not," I said.

"She's dead," he said. "We all got cards about it from her mother. There was an accident at the factory. She fell into the glue vat. I'm sorry. I thought for sure you'd know." We sat together. A television somewhere in the distance was playing a rerun of some talk show from the booming eighties. Tom Lehman struggled to his feet, took a whiz, zipped up haphazardly, shook my shaking hand with his wet hand, and went. I didn't get a chance to tell him I was dying.

By the urine of Tom Lehman I sat down and wept. That's when I saw Lisa. She came back to me, appeared in the evening air behind the bar and hung there like a vision, her long black hair rippling with something more than ordinary energy. She didn't say anything, but she was smiling, and her smile came to me as a gift and not as a humiliation. I didn't need to watch the buffalo gallop away, which is a euphemism for being humiliated that is popular among the American Indians. Lisa looked like something I needed but

17

could never have. She always looked that way. In her left hand, there was something circular and white; as I moved closer, I saw that it was a commemorative plate, with a picture of Merv Griffin and a simple inscription: "1925–2011: Served His Country Well." Merv looked great on the plate. He didn't look a day over seventy. He smiled, benign and wise, his silver hair shining like an altarpiece, and then the plate began to rise out of Lisa's hand. It rose until it was even with her head, and kept rising, until it was over her like a sun or a moon. Simple, floating, it was the last thing I saw.

NOTES ON REVISING LAST NIGHT'S DREAM

Talking parrot needs to lose Ricky Ricardo accent.

Old girlfriend who has moved on to date other men should not look so beautiful.

Replace man wearing black hat (trite!) with woman wearing red shoes (cinematic!).

Tibet has no stock-car racing.

Knife next to breakfast plate need not bloom into flowers.

PAINT IT SHIMMERING CORAL

LONDON (Reuters) - Rock legend Mick Jagger has applied to the European Union to register "Mick Jagger'" as a trademark for more than 20 items, British newspapers reported Wednesday. They included eau de cologne, deodorant, fingernail treatments, footwear and headgear. The Express newspaper quoted a spokesman for Jagger as saying the application had been made simply to prevent other people from using the veteran rocker's name to promote products. "He did not sit at home and think 'How can I market a new lip-gloss?'" the spokesman said.

"How can I market a new lip-gloss?" thought Mick Jagger as he sat at home. The television was showing a program that seemed to be about the history of aviation, but might have been about the social lives of ants. Jagger wasn't certain of the topic of the program, mainly because he had the sound on the television down, and the sound on his stereo turned up. The stereo was playing "Satisfaction," a song he had written that had recently been named the top rock song of the century. Truth be told, Jagger was not even really watching the television, but looking rather fixedly at a mirror he had mounted over the television, and looking more specifically at his own reflection in the mirror. His reflection was moving its lips to the words of the song: "Can't be a man," he sang, "'cause he doesn't smoke the same cigarettes as me." Those are lips, Jagger thought, that could launch a thousand tubes of gloss.

It wasn't until a few minutes had passed that Jagger began to reconsider the idea that gloss, launched or otherwise, came in tubes. Perhaps gloss came in congealed, oleaginous sticks, or perhaps it was simply applied to the lips with a small brush. This question perplexed him for ten minutes, which was like a kind of eternity. He supposed it was because he was tired: He had been up all night, dancing in front of the mirror while he listened to his old records. He had been inspired by the victory of "Satisfaction" in the poll of the century's best songs, and initially he had intended merely to play it once and be done with it. But something, perhaps nostalgia but perhaps not, had reared itself up inside him, rejuvenated him, and he had gone on and on into the night, singing "19th Nervous Breakdown," "Mother's Little Helper," "Let It Bleed," even donning his Baron Samedi hat and taking up his voodoo cane and performing "Sympathy for the Devil." It wasn't until early morning that he thought of the lip-gloss—this was the strange thing; and what was strange was that he had spent all night looking at his own lips in the mirror, but never once thought how much better they would look decorated with a gloss. And if his lips could be improved by gloss, then why not the lips of the world, which he figured to be roughly twice as many as the number of people in the world, though he supposed that there were some people somewhere with single lips, or without any lips at all. Poor bastards, he thought, and turned off the television.

It is true that sometimes a flare of inspiration will simply burn in the sky and then fall smoking to the ground; it is also true that sometimes that same flare will drift over water, and its light will be reflected, and, in that reflection, magnified. Such was Jagger's thinking, more or less, as he let his mind settle on the prospect of producing a lip-gloss, for no sooner had it settled that it was moving again, moving into thoughts of eau de cologne, deodorant, fingernail treatments, footwear, and even headgear. The eu de cologne would have to have a scent of distinction twined around something mysterious. The deodorant would be subtle, of course. The footwear could communicate the youth that remains strong on into old age. What would unite these products, of course, would be their quality, and their elegance, and their implicit wit, but more than that it would be the Jagger name. Jagger suddenly remembered that he had a lawyer, that, in fact, he had dozens of lawyers. Surely one of those lawyers knew how to trademark his name so that he could begin to create lip-glosses and footwear. Maybe one of those lawyers was a lady lawyer who might know whether or not gloss came in a tube. Yes, he thought, looking into the mirror again—but this time not the mirror mounted over the television, which had temporarily fallen out of favor as the result of an unfortunate point of light that was traveling across the television room, but rather a smaller pocket mirror he carried for emergencies—this would be a wonderful plan, a plan capable of producing not just additional wealth and fame, but something more elusive: satisfaction.

FRAGMENTS FROM *MICROSOFT! THE MUSICAL*

For a time, no one was more famous than Bill Gates. Not you. Not me. But even as he built one of the most formidable business empires in the history of Western Civilization, Gates earned a reputation for being, well, a bit wormy. One night, Bill Gates came to me in a dream. He was wearing nothing but his underwear. I call these kinds of dreams "nightmares." This particular nightmare was rendered somewhat less horrible by the fact that the Bill Gates in my dream had a lovely singing voice. When I awoke, I found that I could not forget the songs with which the dream Bill Gates had serenaded me. I know that Professor Onge has suggested that he was somehow responsible for encouraging me to write this first musical, but I can find no record of the letter he claims to have sent in which he urges me to "pen satiric verse about the major figures of the day." The only correspondence from that period, in fact, is a postcard he mailed from Paris on which he had doodled a small Eiffel tower surrounded by a constellation of berets.

—B.G.

*   *   *

FRAGMENTS FROM *MICROSOFT! THE MUSICAL*

{MICHELLE, a Microsoft drone, sends an email to her supervisor.}

I have come to your attention
As a candidate for mention
Or for promotion.
Pacific Ocean
Waves are not larger than my devotion.

{MICHELLE, rebuffed by her supervisor, seeks out CHAIRMAN BILL GATES in the company cafeteria.}

I had a hunch
You eat your lunch
In this facility.

Please Mr. Chairperson
If you're a fair person
Reward my ability.

{GATES denounces MICHELLE.}

Get out of my sight.
Begone, begone.
The king has the right.
To crush every pawn.

How will I have

Your position filled?
I know!
I'll build a
Version two
Point oh
Of you!

{MICHELLE laments her humiliation.}

Working for this corporation
Is roughly equal to castration.
Or, to speak with more precision,
Painful female circumcision.

{MICHELLE devotes herself to ruining GATES by seducing him.}

I once met a guy who designed an operating system,
So I kissed him.
I once met a guy who designed an input-output device,
So I was nice.
Now baby, close the Windows and close the door.
You know what I came here for.
I've worked my way around the town
And it ain't just the network that's going down.

{GATES falls in love with MICHELLE.}

Subroutine,
I think of you as a subroutine.

What does that mean?
It means that you compute.
I wish that I had learned to play the lute.

Circuitry,
I long to inspect your circuitry.
I feel so free
To say that you compute.
You fit me much better than an anti-trust suit.

*{MICHELLE leads GATES on and then dumps him. He is
heartbroken.}*

You say that we'll be breaking up
But the morning sun that's waking up
Seems to contradict you, darling,
And the starling's lovely song
Also says you're wrong.
If my heart is part of your heart,
If I am indeed your secret twin,
Then how on Earth can you bear to see me
Inside that great Recycling Bin?

*{GATES cashes in a substantial part of his fortune, takes a
leave of absence from his duties, and follows MICHELLE across
the country.}*

It has been an uphill battle
Ever since I left Seattle.

Oh, brave city, rainy
But true.
Oh fluorescents that are
Hard on the eyes.
I may be brainy
And wealthy
But I'm stupid, unhealthy,
and certainly far from wise,
For losing you!

{MICHELLE grows to love GATES. They returns to Seattle and marry. Eventually, GATES gives MICHELLE her promotion.}

THE END

SNAPSHOT

Mr. Greenman, as I have written elsewhere, has an interest in the Russian writers. For this, I am thankful, because their sense of consequence is unimpeachable. When I knew Mr. Greenman as a younger man, he had developed an admiration, but not a fondness, for such giants as Dostoevsky, Gogol, and Tolstoy. His fondness was reserved for the younger generation: for Sasha Sokolov and particularly for Grigory Satyrenko, a student of Sokolov's with whom Mr. Greenman corresponded for many years. This story, "Snapshot," strikes me as a fraternal twin to Satyrenko's middle-period novella "In Here, There Is a Shell," developing the same themes of photographic truth and photographic deception; in both cases, the camera as an instrument that inscribes as well as describes. While many of Mr. Greenman's works are content to mystify, this is one of the rare works that endeavors to satisfy. To attempt a pun: It is fully developed. I only regret the fact that the singing in this story has such a limited role—when Pyotor Petrovich's son hums a snatch of a popular tune, he is articulating a need that lives in all of us.   —L.O.

* * *

It is April. In Moscow, the cherry blossoms are in bloom, and fleecy boughs canopy the flat grey streets. One morning, over his toast and coffee, Pyotor Petrovich reads of a dispute between American and British researchers played out in the pages of *The London Journal of Scientific Inquiry*. A distinguished British physicist has challenged the unorthodox results of an American team, insinuating that he is not satisfied with the soundness of their laboratory methods. Pyotor Petrovich is a conscientious man, and this sort of thing upsets him greatly. When he was a young graduate student, his mentor, the esteemed Doctor Alexsandr Rostikov, was infamous for the scornful gaze he would fix upon students remiss in their experimental preparations. Rostikov would tower over the helpless tyro, and then, from the Andean peak of his unimpeachable intelligence, issue a single scathing word: "Careless!" Pyotor Petrovich only needed one such incident to terrify him, and to convince him of the absolute necessity of meticulous order, both within the scientist and in the environment around him. "We are caretakers of new realities," Pyotor Petrovich often explains to his younger colleagues, his rhetoric and delivery altogether less magisterial than Rostikov's, but every bit as heartfelt. "The experiment is a world, and its Genesis must be seamless. What happens afterward, we cannot say. We can only watch. The apple may be plucked and eaten. The apple may be left untouched. After the setup, we are a perfect eye. But during the setup, we are the one and only God." This deistic metaphor rarely finds favor among the younger researchers, who view it as a quaint myth of impossible exactitude, but even they agree that procedural prudence is vital.

Pyotor Petrovich's initial suspicions regarding the *London Journal* case, which arise during his breakfast, are only confirmed by his second reading, which takes place on the bus from his flat to Drudzgrad-7, the secret research city just south of the capital, and his third, which occurs while he is waiting to enter the I-9 Lab. The Britisher, it seems, is trying to return to prominence after nearly a decade of relative invisibility, and the upstart group of young researchers from Baltimore has had the misfortune of serving as the first victims of this renewed vigor. Not only because he tends to side with the underdogs—it is in Pyotor Petrovich's nature to support some notion of universal parity, where all benefits and deficits are subtly counterweighed—but because of the clear facts of the controversy, which he reviews as he eats his modest lunch of cheese and onion, that he finds himself growing increasingly incensed at what he perceives as unjust treatment of the Americans. In at least one section of his challenge, this Englishman has resorted to irresponsible conjecture regarding the execution of a Hungarian experiment of 1978, and this egregious misreading of the Rackozy setup invalidates his entire argument. Pyotor Petrovich hopes the Americans are aware of this flaw in the attack, but he has his doubts—few men in the world, he knows, are as attentive to these minute details of operations as he is. Greatly agitated, he paces his small office space, all the while ticking a fingernail across the rim of his styrofoam coffee cup, and then, in a quite uncharacteristic outburst, banging a closed fist against the flat white formica of his lab table. "This is true injustice!" he exclaims loudly. Natalya Azkharava, the thick brunette in charge of equipment requisitioning, looks up from her desk and gazes quizzically through the glass partition. Pyotor Petrovich returns an abashed smile. But all afternoon, as he fits lenses and samples wavelengths, he cannot help thinking of the team of four Americans, and how they must be clustered around a conference table in The Johns Hopkins University, picking nervously at cold meats and vegetables as they draft and redraft letters of protest. "We the undersigned wish to object strenuously to the charges of our distinguished colleague…" "It is with great certitude that we reassert our original results and urge the withdrawal of this unwarranted criticism…" "We appeal to the fairness and objectivity of the international community…"

From the top drawer of his desk, Pyotor Petrovich withdraws his prized fountain pen—he ordered it years before from a French catalog, and was overjoyed when it met and even exceeded the beauty of the model pictured in the advertisement—and writes to Dr. L. Rashman, the lead researcher on the American study. Pyotor Petrovich is very proud of his English, almost as proud as he is of his pen. He had spent some time in London as a student during the Fifties, and attended a play starring Jean Simmons, something about a young boy imprisoned in a manor house by his beautiful but tyrannical aunt. After the play, he stood outside on Shaftesbury Avenue with the crowds, waiting for Simmons to emerge, and when she did, he extended his playbill to her deferentially. He kept the program, the actress's name scrawled in two hurried tiers across its face, and when he returned from London presented it to his fianceé as a gift, along with a love note in fluent English. It is with that same English—weakened slightly, of course, by the intervening decades, but still more than adequate—that he writes to the American doctor in condolence and commiseration. "Doctor Rashman, I know how great must be your discomfort," he writes in a careful script, his lower lip folded inward with concentration. "I am research scientist here in Russia and an associate of the late Doctor Alexsandr Rostikov, with whom you are perhaps familiar. I studied under him years ago. In reading the *London Journal of Scientific Inquiry*, I have looked at an article about your research team what I feel is most unjust. Please send to me a copy of your original article. I would like to read of your work and then to write on your behalf to those who I know. Also, that you would read the 1978 paper delivered by G. Rackozy in Budapest, and that you would see the errors of Dr. Phillips in applying it to this case. I sense that you are in the right, and hope to help convince others of this." After signing his name, Pyotor Petrovich rereads the letter, and feeling that he has assumed a tone at once too condescending and too pessimistic, adds a light-hearted postscript: "I wish that you will accept my humble assistance, and hope that you are not a rash man."

After sealing the letter in a crisp envelope of watery green color, Pyotor Petrovich deposits it in a red wire basket on the far right of his desk. The basket is situated just in front of a photograph of his wife, long-dead, and his two sons, who are grown now and live nearby. Behind those photographs are more: another of his wife as a young bride, his sons playing in the snow, him and Anna on holiday. He has practiced this hobby of amateur photography for more than thirty years, and his persistence has rewarded him with countless photographs of his family and friends and none at all of himself. In the one photograph in which Pyotor Petrovich should appear, a lab snapshot that shows him working with Rostikov, his face is obscured by a beaker perched upon a ringstand. According to his own record, he is an ontological naught; he often jokes that if he were to vanish, it would be without a trace. And yet, a discerning eye would find evidence of him everywhere. In the careful maintenance of the lab's lasers; in the white coat, right cuff rubbed with ink, that hangs upon the corner hook; in the apple and the pastry missing from the Drudzgrad-7 commissary every afternoon. And even in the pictures themselves, in the way the faces of the subjects reach across the photographic plane and locate him with love.

The advancing spring is regressing dawn, and bringing the first few rays of light to the early morning hours. Pyotor Petrovich lives in a small flat that he has rented with prompt monthly payments for the nine years since his wife's death. A tiny corner kitchen, a sofa that folds out into a bed, and a large mahogany bookshelf. They are mostly his wife's books; she was a poet, and she collected other poets in thin brown volumes, Akhmatova, Tsvetaeva, Mandelstam. Each morning he rises at half-past five, washes down flavorless toast with lukewarm coffee, and then walks to the corner to catch the government bus into the research park. He is usually among the first to arrive at his building, and he awaits the opening of the Checkpoint Alexei security gate along with the other obsessively punctual chemists and botanists, astrophysicists and physicists. The men who gather in the early morning arrange themselves into informal fours and fives, and wonder aloud about the condition of the country, especially the rapid change that is occurring in the national rhetoric. Pyotor Petrovich himself has a set of stock comments, most of which are cut with the cautionary saws of folk tales; Gorbachev is both the prince and the fool, or change is a golden ball coveted by an avaricious empress. The aeronautics engineers who work the East Wing are the least agreeable to these impromptu conferences—a close-knit group of tall and haughty men susceptible to affectations, monocles, and pocket-watch chains, they are not native Russians, but the sons of German exiles who came East as defectors in the wake of the Nazi downfall. Their labs reflect their otherness, and are arranged with forbidding Kopfverdreher precision, instruments tagged and sorted, circles chalked on the countertops to indicate the proper storage zones for instruments.

Pyotor Petrovich, by contrast, approaches his work as a natural extension of his life, continuous with his domestic existence, and as a result, his laboratory is decorated like the modest home of a cottager—like his own home, in fact. Lab equipment and scientific paperwork are juxtaposed haphazardly with chance articles of cheap furniture—a compact cubic refrigerator and a red velour easy chair, a weatherbeaten mahogany end-table, and a wall-mounted plywood shelf that holds volumes of Pushkin, Flaubert, and his beloved Dostoevsky. This shelf overhangs a small metal workbench at the rear of the lab, and it is Pyotor Petrovich's sanctum. For more than a decade now, he has been collecting castaway parts from neighboring labs and cobbling together inventions, experimenting with small advances in electronics and optical technology. The previous summer, for instance, he had begun work on a perfectly flat video monitor, thin as card stock, and he had recently drafted plans for a portrait camera equipped with an automatic framing feature. Almost none of these devices works correctly—the video monitor, for instance, can display only one image per second, rendering it insufficient for anything but novelty status—but this does not worry Pyotor Petrovich. In fact, it is the very failure of his inventions to function that engages him. Imperfect, incapable, unresolved, they inspire in him a sentiment that transcends pragmatic concerns; they are like children who will never grow up, and will always need the guiding hand of a parent to find their way in the world. The longer he spends tinkering with their circuits without definitive results, the more affection he feels for them. They need him.

It is an overcast day, threatening yet another May rain, when Pyotor Petrovich receives a manila envelope in the mail. It is three weeks after he has sent his letter to Johns Hopkins—he has been waiting eagerly for a response—and his heart thrills when he sees that the envelope is posted with an American stamp, a watercolor of the Wright brothers at Kitty Hawk. Before he even opens the envelope, he razors off its post-corner; he must show this stamp to the aeronautics engineers. This is who they have to thank, not their Venckmanns and von Brauns. For a letter-opener, he uses a dull butter knife, sawing away at the flap until he finally extracts a neatly folded sheet of stationery. It is white but not white, and he holds it against the formica top to better gauge its color. Cream. The letter is from Dr.

Rashman, and it is forthright and friendly, exactly as he imagines America:

> Dear Dr. Petrovich, I thank you very much for your interest in our case. I am happy to inform you that we have reached an understanding with Dr. Phillips, and that he has ceased to hint at improprieties. He has not yet apologized for casting aspersions, but as a colleague of mine has remarked, we're not holding our breath. Still, the last few weeks have been difficult, sometimes maddeningly so, and I cannot tell you how much I appreciate the support of colleagues across the globe. I was especially intrigued to learn of your association with Doctor Rostikov, whose work provided the foundation for so much of my own. We scientists work too often with theoretical propositions, isolated from phenomenal fact, and though I have seen countless photographs of the man, I never until now conceived of him as an actual corporeal being, someone with students and friends. If for nothing else, I thank you for helping to give a certain heft to my professional imaginations.

The final paragraph is short, but despite its brevity Pyotor Petrovich has to read it a few times to be certain that he has understood: *In response to your wonderful postscript, I must admit that I am not a rash man. In fact, I am not a man at all. Yours, Dr. Lila Rashman.* A woman. He never would have guessed, and yet now that he knows he is not surprised.

The American has enclosed an article about the resolution of the conflict, the opposing parties making a public show of goodwill at an international conference held in New York City. Alongside the article, the journal has printed a photograph of the Hopkins team, all of them smiling broadly and one of them, a stout fiftyish woman, gripping the hand of the Englishman. Pyotor Petrovich searches the caption, and is relieved to learn that this is not Doctor Rashman. He finds her finally in the left foreground, standing behind a table. She is a tall woman with long black hair and a penetrating gaze, and she looks rather young, no older than thirty-five. A slight warmth rises into his face. The photograph does not flatter her entirely—there is something thick and rectangular about the set of her jaw—but this Pyotor Petrovich chalks up to the cruelty of the camera. He knows how it can falsify; his wife, slight and small, always looked slightly overweight in photographs, with an overbite his sympathetic gaze could not detect.

He mounts the photograph on the wall over his workbench. As the afternoon proceeds, he comes to understand it better. Some of the heaviness of her face results from the shadow cast by the figure to her left, a well-known Harvard mathematician whose name he cannot recall now. And while the woman is older than he initially suspected—at least forty, he now guesses—he can see her twentieth year in the playful tilt of her head, her tenth in the unguarded brilliance of her smile. But it is her eyes that draw him most powerfully, with such a luminosity that looking into them, even through the intervening medium of the photograph, is like listening to the voice of their owner. The magic of this photograph, and of photographs in general, lies in the multiplicity of their effect, the way they operate both viscerally and surreptitiously, simultaneously presenting a simulacrum of reality to the intellect and floating undetected into the recesses of the mind (memory, desire) like wisps of fragrance from a bakery window. Anyone could look at this picture and fall in love with this woman instantly. Pyotor Petrovich does. And yet, there is a certain gravity that dilates this process. Gazing into Lila Rashman's eyes, which he imagines from their amplitudes are green, Pyotor Petrovich feels quite acutely the pain of his wife's loss. One thing has nothing to do with the other, and yet perhaps they are the same—this new beautiful face renewing an old wound of the heart, and especially the memory of another woman, also quite beautiful, who is now long hid among packs of years.

Every night, Pyotor Petrovich sits down to write at the simple pine desk in his apartment. As a young man, he believed that scheduled reflection yielded profoundly therapeutic benefits, and that a mere hour of meditative jotting each day returned to a man many more hours of spiritual equilibrium. Some nights he spends with his journal; on others he composes letters to old friends, or transcribes sections of Pushkin. Tonight, with the light spray of the May rain descending, Pyotor Petrovich writes to Lila Rashman.

He discusses scientific issues, including the most recent American advances in laser optics and how they might profitably be applied to medical technology. The letter doubles as a language lesson. Pyotor Petrovich, whose confidence in his English has been tempered by the American doctor's effortlessly elegant prose, has asked his new corespondent to correct his errors, and to be unflinching in her criticism. He encourages her with a number of purposeful solecisms, "After a hard day of work I am exhaust," and "It is to you that I make question." She finds these, and more. Her grammatical rigor kindles a sort of camaraderie.

And yet, it is not only the grammar. The letters have an indisputable appeal, and they produce a bright excitement that sometimes flowers into joy. Pyotor Petrovich, a man not given to jocosity, finds himself humming a ballad from his student days under his breath. "The river and the afternoon, your arm at rest in mine…" He has quite forgotten the rest of the words, although he knows at some point the couple rests in a deep green grove, at which point the boy carves the name of his beloved in the trunk of a young pine. Whenever he had sung the song before, the lovers' circumstance drew Pyotor Petrovich into curious reverie. Were the names still on the tree? Did surface carvings move upward along the trunk as the tree grew in height? Were they covered by the addition of new rings? But this particular morning, as he hums with Lila Rashman in mind, he finds himself suddenly liberated from this line of inquiry, which strikes him as extending well beyond the purview of the tune, and he concentrates instead on the music itself—the periodic rise and fall of the melody, the way that the notes of the chorus cluster in bunches like grapes, the perfect correspondence between the trilling coda and his own lightsome mood. A bumblebee of wadded tape and paper buzzes on the flat top of the file cabinet. He gathers it into his right hand and flings it toward the wastepaper basket, smiling abstractly as it caroms off the rim.

One Monday afternoon, shortly after the weather has thickened in the summer heat, Pyotor Petrovich's older son Vasily comes to visit him at the laboratory. To other men, the two of them must seem quite similar; there is a striking physical resemblance, the same collapsed chin and sharp dark features, the eyes that are the glossy brown of seacoast pebbles. And yet, as men of the world, they could not be more different. As a boy, Vasily had been intelligent but impatient, driven by a burning desire for change that sometimes bordered on despair. As a man, he has become a big wheel in the fledgling world of Soviet advertising, a key figure in the transition from one type of propaganda to the next. Attired like a sharpster in a Botany 500 suit and brushed suede shoes, he is all rude shift, as if a pea has been slipped beneath the mattress of his life. He is a rash man. But his energy is contagious, and his rough manner cannot conceal how much he loves his father.

"Ah, so this is your American doctor," Vasily says, tapping the photo, whistling too loudly. "Very easy on the eyes. It's what they call a cocoa tan. I'll bet she has smooth hands and nice curves. The complexion-and-contour model is all the rage in America these days."

"I have been in communication with her about a very important case for the international research community. You see, a well-respected British scientist accused her team of misconduct."

Vasily is uninterested. "Yah, yah."

"The matter is quite serious, I assure you."

"But this picture is more serious to me. Do you deny that she is bewitching? And if you do deny, perhaps you could explain to me why you have put the picture up? Is it covering a hole in the wall?"

"I have a picture of your mother in that same pose."

"What pose? There's no pose in that photography. It's a straight-on head shot." But his son was not looking carefully. Pyotor Petrovich had studied the photograph enough times to recall it in great detail, and he envisioned her left hand, with its long nails, hovering over the back of the chair, the penumbral rim along the lower edge of her knuckles suggesting a distance of inches between the fingers and the furniture. The picture was taken at a slight angle—the window in the room's rear, which admitted a torrent of white light, was not level with the photographic frame—and the conference table that anchored the scene was novelly foreshortened. A clock on the left wall reads nine.

"I will create an ad campaign for your laboratory. Hop on over to the Drudzgrad-7 Institute. Watch tomorrow's lasers through magic spectacles." He has a great persuasive energy, even though his own conviction is clearly evanescent, and the trained observer in Pyotor Petrovich recognizes the pilgrim under the cynic, the eagerness and even the naiveté in his son's brittle wit. At fifteen, Vasily had travelled to Sofia, and the letters he sent home had convinced Anna that her son was destined to be a great writer. "I am happier than ever," he wrote, "and more uncomfortable than ever. Once your life has taken on the shape of magic, you cannot wait patiently for each individual miracle." Pyotor Petrovich wishes he could warn Vasily of the dangers of his attitude, the folly of embracing extravagant hope, but the thought of his wife softens him. "They are not spectacles," he tells his son, "but special lenses crafted for the testing of new optical technologies."

"You speak like an old woman. The word we print next to it, that is what the world accepts as genuine. Phrase is power." When Pyotor Petrovich announces that he must return to his work, Vasily salutes. "Right, old bean," he says, camouflaging his disappointment with an insincere chipperness. "Do hope to speak with you again some time soon." That night, as he reviews the visit, what surfaces within Pyotor Petrovich is not the barbed comments or the accents, but a single gentle image of Vasily singing, applying a wavery tenor to a popular tune that has drifted over from Prague or Budapest, and before that probably from the West:

> *To kiss a second pair of lips*
> *I know it is a vice*
> *but tell me true what would you do*
> *when she's half as far and twice as nice?*

* * *

The next morning, Pyotor Petrovich phones his younger son Jurij, who agrees to visit him in the early afternoon. Once a quiet boy with none of the arrogance of his brother—as a child he had been the very model of modesty and kindness—Jurij has become moody, and sometimes almost inexplicably so, in the last four or five years. Since Anna's death, Pyotor Petrovich knows, the family has endured a vague and general estrangement; in a society of men it is inevitable that any individual will feel distant from the fears and hopes of the others, and even from those of his own heart. At times, Vasily has tried to serve the maternal role, calling the three of them together in a rude burlesque of Anna's gossamer diplomacy, and Jurij has resisted those attempts. But this is something different.

Jurij is a concert violinist with one of the finest suburban symphonies, and his music is the most brilliant hue in the spectrum of his young life, a piercing sunflower yellow. At the time of Anna's death, he had just completed his own musical training, and was planning to join the staff of an academy for young prodigies. Anna thought this decision suited him perfectly. "He loves young children so much," she told Pyotor Petrovich, "and is so gentle with them." But after five years at the school, Jurij suddenly submitted his resignation. He was marrying another teacher, a cellist, and the following year, they had a daughter. If Jurij seemed to enjoy his family life at first, there were soon signs of discontent, a bitter gauntness in his manner. Pyotor Petrovich was bothered by this, but he was most troubled by Jurij's growing aversion to Vasily. Whereas he once respected his brother immensely, his attitude now alternated between disdain and envy, and in Vasily's presence he wore a continual sneer that gave him the appearance of a boy on the verge of tears. In the last year or so—since a particularly peevish outburst in which Jurij disparaged Vasily as a "mountebank" and a "rug salesman"—the two had seen each other only rarely, and Pyotor Petrovich did not have the strength to force a reconciliation.

Today, Jurij seems talkative, which Pyotor Petrovich accounts as a positive sign until he begins to listen more closely to the content of his son's conversation. It seems he is thinking of leaving Moscow. "I am considering Petersburg," he says, "or perhaps Paris. Somewhere with a well-respected orchestra and some distance from this place. Perhaps that way I can concentrate on my music. These days, when I play, I feel that I am doing nothing but planting myself deeper in mediocrity and sadness." The previous winter, Jurij and his wife had lost a child at twenty weeks, and the miscarriage had strained the marriage greatly. Through Jurij, whose oblique remarks were often quite direct, Pyotor Petrovich gathered that his son suspected Mariana of infidelity, and that he was protecting himself from the consequences by conducting an affair himself.

"Mediocrity?" Pyotor Petrovich says, thinking of Anna, wondering if she monitored the three of them, crisp surveillance pictures delivered to her study in the afterlife. "Nonsense. I've copied out all the praiseworthy bits from last month's Tchaikovsky: 'Impeccable tone,' 'the picture of delicate intensity,' 'the performer's artful domination of the audience.' I even have a picture from the newspaper. There, behind you, to the left of the workbench." Looking at the photograph, Pyotor Petrovich hears the orchestra, the swooping group adagios, the pizzacato of his son's passion singing on the strings. It is hard for him, he admits, to connect that man with the one who stands before him, and harder still to connect either of them with the happy infant who used to gurgle and pinch roundly at his arms. The changes in Jurij these days are like strokes of an oar across the smoky top of a winter lake.

Over the next weeks, his visits become more frequent

and more erratic—sometimes a ten-minute chat early in the morning, other times a long and silent appearance that spans the afternoon. One day he stays late, and as he stares at his father with an inscrutable look, Pyotor Petrovich feels as if he were being observed by the ocelli of a peacock. While Vasily is incessant in his commentary—"For the want of a loaf," he might say, tipping *Crime and Punishment* from its station on the bookshelf—Jurij notices nothing, not even the picture of Lila Rashman that counterbalances the picture of him. One day, he asks his father for a camera. This request animates Pyotor Petrovich at once; not only does the mere mention of the device transport him into the past, where he is greeted by dutiful and happy children and a lovely wife, but Jurij's request gives him the opportunity to hold forth on his newest invention. With a happy laugh, he produces a small black box, no larger than a cigarette pack, with a panel of buttons stretching across its top. This is the plain-paper camera, a device that transfers black-and-white photographs to ordinary white paper in the manner of a xerographic copier. He has had great success with it late-ly—though the images produced are of inferior quality, the process compensates with its incredibly low cost—and has begun to dream of marketing it, rueing his dreams of wealth even as he dreams them, knowing how foolish they must be. "I hope that it brings you pleasure," says Pyotor Petrovich, proffering the camera with a flourish. His son returns a grim indecipherable smile.

With his only promising invention loaned out, Pyotor Petrovich wraps himself tighter in his epistolary flirtation, feeling as he did when he was a young man. He pulls a footstool into the closet and retrieves from a high shelf a box of stationery, a gift to him from his wife in the year of her death. The beautiful golden hue of the paper has since faded, but it has left behind a pattern, a comfortable honeyed grain. It is proper, and even generous, to write his letters on this paper. It will remind him of his strongest moments, and help him validate them.

Lila. He writes it and then stops. He paces his apartment, singing, the freshness of the music almost indecent, like the sharp sweet swell of a newly mown meadow. In Britain he once developed a passion for a radio singer named Lily Atamasco, but this is an unfamiliar variation. Lila. He pronounces it sometimes in bed as a private enjoyment, feeling quite silly, but attempting the American accents, elongating the *i* until it is a long staircase of gentle grade and the *l*'s newels at either end, with the *a* an exhaled afterthought, a foot carpet thrown by the bottom-most riser. Spoken in the dark of his bedroom, a close and treacly dark more green than black, her name is a stream, cool and subtle, purling in his throat. Lila. Under the spell of these two syllables, each the imperfect copy of the other, together a perfect pair, his work begins to change. He is less methodical and less patient, finds himself daydreaming in ways he has not in forty years—hung up on a vague memory of the first line of "Novogodnee," an unfamiliar raven-haired figure glimpsed from behind—and then finds the daydreams alternating with flashes of brilliant intuition. What would Rostikov think? Would he scorn this intuitive turn as sophistry and sorcery? When Pyotor Petrovich attempts the mental transport that usually brings him closer to the man, his memory is of a portly figure rather pontifical than authoritative, and with an affected orotundity that verges on the comical. One night he dreams that he portrays his old mentor in a skit, and that he waxes the ends of his costume moustache until his eyes are wet with laughing tears. He knows he is performing for someone, that he is showing off, and when he wakes in the morning he can do nothing but lie grinning in his bed. The dreamer and the scientist are warring within him, and victory is falling to the dreamer.

It is early on a Tuesday morning when Jurij calls the flat. "Father," he says, and nothing else. Pyotor has not even had his toast and coffee.

"Jurij," he says. No response. He repeats his son's name, searches for him in the interminable silence. Still nothing. His heart thudding, Pyotor Petrovich sighs to calm himself and delivers a sugared homily. "Jurij, listen to me. Whatever is troubling you, it will pass. You are very young still, and look upon such difficulties as permanent. I have more experience with these things. Please, Jurij, I cannot talk to you now. The bus for work is leaving shortly. But come by and see me this afternoon."

Finally, Jurij answers. "I will." But Pyotor waits into the evening, staring at the wall clock and the newspaper photo of Jurij beneath it, and finally leaves shortly after seven. The next day Ivan Zaitsev, the lab director, informs him that the equipment office cannot account for a small amount of money. It has been accounted as lost, but there are suspicions of theft, directed chiefly at Old Ganev, who has guided his mop listlessly around the corners of the lab for almost twenty years now. It is only later, when he returns to his small apartment, that he remembers Jurij's phone call, and feels a sick tug at his stomach as he wonders if perhaps his younger son subscribes to a very different standard of conduct from that which he has upheld all his life.

*   *   *

Two weeks later—weeks that have passed without any sign of Jurij, who continues to schedule visits he does not keep—a small fire breaks out in a laboratory down the hall, and spreads through I-9. Arriving in the morning, Pyotor Petrovich finds one of the Kopfverdrehers clucking in the security area. "What's the matter?" he asks, and is answered only by stern Teutonic silence. In his lab, a sooty patina has settled over the floor and workbench. His bookshelf attests to a critical precision in the flames' encroachment; the Dostoevsky is damaged, but the Puskhin barely touched. It is not until nine that he notices his greatest loss—the two newsprint photographs that flanked his workbench are gone, and where they hung there are now only nails ringed by collars of carbonized paper. He finds a single scrap that must have been blown free of the flames and handles it as reverently as the palmer treats his leaves. She is not in it, only the face of a man who stood to her rear right, but he knows her in the man's aspect. That night, he writes with greater urgency, heedless of his grammar and dependent on his intensity to navigate him safely through. He reports the fire, even ventures an explanation that he will admit to no one else—"I am afraid that my son is somehow involved in the cause"—and concludes with a request divested of his usual playful manner. "My dear Doctor Rashman, I would like from you a replacement of the photograph. Or else I should feel as if there is nothing firm beneath my feet."

Another round of vists by his sons. Again, Vasily comes first, volume turned high, pressuring his father to help him invest in a new business. "Oh, that's right, father. You don't know what business is. How could you? When have you seen true industry at work? The hot blood of capital flowing freely."

He hardly has the energy to spar, but he makes a valiant attempt, fearful that if he does not, Vasily will sense his preoccupation, and ferret out its source. "I was once a visitor in Berlin."

"Ach, Berlin. Jelly doughnuts. I am speaking of America. Bruce Springsteen. Michael Jackson. Julia Roberts. Abundancies you cannot dream of. Once more, into the broil. Your ideas will make us men thick with money." From his tone, it is apparent that it is more than mere cupidity that powers this vision of a life transformed. It is pride in his father, and it is love.

Shortly after Vasily departs, singing another American song, Jurij arrives. He enters without ceremony, Pyotor Petrovich's camera extended before him, and despite the shaky smile on his face, his struggle with his demons has apparently been to lamentable purpose, for he looks dissipated and afraid, with a terrible unevenness to his gaze. Shortly after he arrives he bends over the wastebasket and spits noisily into its depths, an insanity. "Father," he says, and then pauses, steadying himself against the workbench.

His smile is gone now and his starched shirt collar pretends to cut his throat. "I have two favors to ask."

"Yes."

"What I need," he resumes, "is for you to hold something for me." He produces a thin manila envelope. "This contains some extremely important documents that need safekeeping until next month." Pyotor Petrovich accepts the envelope without comment and, as his son watches, places it in a file drawer. "Good," says Jurij. "Also, I need more money. Do you have some I could borrow?" Pyotor Petrovich silently gestures toward the top drawer of the desk. Jurij slides out a few bills, and conveys them to a front pocket of his pants. There is something in the gesture that strikes Pyotor Petrovich as professional. He does not ask his son questions, but lets him speak, and speak he does, about his wife, how he loves her, how he hopes that his life regains its balance. "And little Julia," he says, "she is growing so quickly that I close my eyes sometimes to keep an image of her. Yesterday I lay on the ground and held her up flying until my arms hurt." The memory brushes his features with a faint happiness, and Pyotor Petrovich remembers how his son had looked at birth, at two, on the first day of school, on his wedding night. Open-mouthed, seemingly on the verge of explaining what it is that troubles him, Jurij suddenly colors a deep red, and then that color, too, drains from his face, and he leaves the lab without speaking.

That night, Pyotor Petrovich writes a long letter to Lila Rashman, a confession of sorts that telescopes his paternity into a few representative incidents—Vasily's birth, a minor ice-skating accident when Jurij was eight, the stark mystery of that afternoon's visit. "I do not know what to do. He will not confide in me, and his fear frightens me terribly. All children must grow, and so, too, have my sons, although as men they are leaving me emptier than ever." He intends this lament as a declaration of love, and after rereading the letter copies it into his journal, so nakedly does it present his feelings. He does not, however, mail it.

The following week he spends his evenings in the laboratory, each night staying later than the one before. He eats less and less, not out of diet any longer but because he is not hungry, and one night he realizes that he is pining over the letter he has not mailed, pining like a schoolboy, and that he will not regain his equilibrium until he knows, in some small way, that Lila Rashman understands the extent of his feelings for her. Thursday night, he is tinkering with the camera when he hears a faint noise somewhere in the building, a distant plashing of glass. Ganev, he thinks to himself. Senile. Should tell Ivan Zaitsev. Pyotor Petrovich returns to the camera, and he is probing in its empty stomach with a tweezer, trying to separate two capacitors, when a terrible scraping fills the room. His glance flies to the peephole. Someone is at the laboratory door. He reaches for the telephone, but the lights are suddenly dimmed, and a streak of grey enters his field of vision. Wild, panicked, he gropes for his glasses, spilling a flask of water onto Jurij's envelope, overturning a lamp, and then incongruously, even delicately, depressing the small red button atop the camera. Click. The image is of an older man, his eyes bright with terror, a scream sliding from between his thin concluding lips. A moment later darkness descends with the speed of a shutter.

*   *   *

Vasily will never forget that night. He had a girl at his apartment, a delicious blonde from the firm, and with the help of two bottles of Rumanian wine, he had divested her of her blouse and begun to explore the thrilling heat seeping from beneath her skirt. Fortune, he remembers thinking, is kissing me once more. And then the phone rang. "I am sorry to bother you at home," said the voice, "but there has been an incident in the Drudzgrad-7 lab."

"My father," said Vasily. "Is he hurt?"

"No," said the detective, and Vasily felt relief mingled with annoyance—if not hurt, then why the disturbance—a relief that was quickly obliterated by the force of the clarification. "He is dead."

At the lab, Vasily wept openly in the room that no longer contained his father's body, the spilled water, the overturned lamp. Why would anyone kill this man? Had his behavior been strange, the detective asked. Not at all, Vasily reponded. But he knew that this was not quite true. His father's behavior had been strange. He had been in love.

In the year since he founded the Stuttgart-based Patersen Camerawerkes, Vasily himself has ripened; he has become an important man with a serious manner, a large office, a larger home, and an imperiously beautiful German fiancée. Many days, he cannot believe the change that time has wrought, and he sneaks away with a secretary. Other days, he patrols the office proudly, especially the lobby area, anchored by a photograph of Pyotor Petrovich retrieved from the X-3 prototype the morning after his death. This photograph—grainier than the prints the cameras now produce, but a respectable predecessor nonetheless—has an appropriately memorial flavor, although no one, not even Vasily, imagines the grisly circumstances of its production.

The company is a great success, one of the largest suppliers of personal cameras in Eastern Europe, and its rise is followed with interest by the international press. Hungry for stories of post-Communist accomplishment amid the myriad examples of fracture and failure, journalists are drawn to Patersen not only by its balance sheet but by the young and charismatic president whose financial success conceals two personal tragedies—the murder of his father and the mysterious death of his brilliant younger brother. Selections from Pyotor Petrovich's journals, made public under Vasily's supervision, often accompany articles; the corporation owes its humanistic philosophy, Vasily insists repeatedly in print, to his father. As the first anniversary of the Stuttgart plant approaches, Vasily asks a young German reporter who has recently written on the company if his paper would be interested in the correspondence between Pyotor Petrovich and an American research scientist. "It's a touching story," he says. "He felt so deeply for her, and they never met. We give all of our employees a week's paid vacation when they are married. Her name was Lila Rashman. I will try to contact her if you like, and give your paper an exclusive."

He felt so deeply for her. How deeply? And did she feel for him? Vasily muses on these questions, framing possible answers, on-the-record answers, as the overseas operator patches him transatlantic, as the American operator retrieves the call, as the secretary in the chemistry department places him on hold, and then she is on the line, a pleasant voice with flattened vowels and a quizzical cast. "This is Lila Rashman." He introduces himself. "My father was a scientist in Moscow. He corresponded with you a few years ago. I wonder if you might remember him."

"Of course I remember your father. We had written to one another a few times, and then his letters stopped. Has something happened? Has he lost his job."

"He has lost more than his job." It is a stupid thing to say, characteristic of his love of cleverness over kindness, and it verges on a cruelty toward this stranger who cares for his dead father. She lets out a soft cry. "You don't mean he's..."

"Yes, I'm afraid so." He has regained control now, his consonants rolling, continental and persuasive, his speech the speech of the man he always knew he would become. "A rather tragic case, something in his laboratory. My father was killed by an intruder. It was very difficult for us at first, but easier now. He spoke often of you."

"Yes," she says. There is still a wariness in her voice. "How strange that you should call me now. I will be in Prague this April for a conference, and I was considering phoning your father."

"Prague," he repeats. "How wonderful. You must come to Stuttgart. You will be my guest."

She arrives just before lunch, accompanied by another American doctor. After a round of introductions, the man excuses himself, reminding her that he must be at the station at seven. She sits in Vasily's office, brushing her skirt nervously, and the two of them begin to talk. She is forty-two, ten years divorced, childless, an avid crossword hobbyist. She loves her work. Her traveling companion is a man who believes she will agree to marry him. She will not. Vasily nods ruefully. "I understand completely," he says. I have an engagement myself that I may be breaking shortly. I have found myself sometimes satisfied with only the shallow portions of myself. My father was murdered and my brother, too, is dead." They eat in the company cafeteria, Vasily making a show of his good rapport with even the lowest employees. "Hello, Karl," he says to the burly cashier. "Is your son's twisted ankle healed? He is a smart boy who should not be playing with the roughnecks." Lila Rashman laughs. Late in the afternoon, after an hour of wine has created a provisional intimacy—an intimacy assisted, they both know, by the fact that they will never again see one another—Vasily asks her if she knew his father loved her. She lifts her eyes to his without answering, and a mix of pain and passion flickers in their middle depths. "Would you like to see a photograph of him?" asks Vasily, and she nods.

He takes her to the lobby; a company photographer is waiting. Lila Rashman stands silent before the showcase, shifting. The main lamp has switched to evening wattage, suffusing the case's contents with a yellow melancholy. "I thought he would look different," she says. As she stares at the photo, Vasily permits himself to stare at her. Even teeth. Long black hair. Complexion and contour. He marvels at his father's boldness; she really is quite beautiful. The photographer arranges the pair before the case and snaps once, twice, a third time, each click accompanied by the pop of a recyclable flashbulb manufactured in the Stuttgart facility. Two of the photos are published the next morning alongside an article about the company's first birthday; Lila Rashman is mentioned in a caption as "a friend and colleague of the late Pyotor Petrovich." There will come a time when nothing is left of the picture but an ashen ghost haunting scraps of newsprint. But for now, forever, the two of them together gaze up as at an altar, into the magnified image, grand in modesty and kindness, of Pyotor Petrovich's dead face.

STUCK ON RED: MY HOPES AND DREAMS DETAILED

I. The first paragraph of a book I hope to one day write:

> I am a wealthy country gentleman. I am also a loaf of bread. How do I reconcile these two disparate and seemingly contradictory existences? Simple: I cut a half-inch off the heels, make a sandwich, and eat it in the grand hall of my grand estate. Servants swarm around me, tending to my needs. One sweeps up the crumbs. "Who would cut both heels?" he says. His voice still bears traces of the mines, which is where he came from. I rescued him. He puts me inside a bread-box and closes the lid. Darkness descends like a curtain. My investments appreciate.

II. The last paragraph of that same book:

"I literally need to know," he said. "Literally. I just need to know. Can you tell me? Is it something you can share?" I could not, and said so.

III. The names of some of the characters:

Red
Louisa
Jake
Dr. Petrancko
Victor Petrancko

IV. The probability that I will finish this book:

20 percent

V. The time it took me to write the first paragraph:

2 minutes, 10 seconds

VI. The time it took me to write the last paragraph:

45 seconds

VII. The time it took me to think of the characters' names:

6 minutes, 25 seconds (I got stuck on "Red")

VIII. The time it took me to decide that the first paragraph and last paragraph belonged to a book I might one day write:

5 minutes

IX. Some places the book might be set:

Chicago, Illinois
Wichita, Kansas
San Diego, California
Denver, Colorado

X. What I will do with the money advanced to me by my publisher if it exceeds one hundred thousand dollars:

Buy a house

XI. What I will do with the money advanced to me by my publisher if it is between twenty thousand dollars and one hundred thousand dollars:

Buy a PT Cruiser

XII. The time it has taken to write this piece thus far:

11 minutes, 20 seconds

XIII. The probability that I will finish this piece:

90 percent

XIV. What I will do if this piece is accepted for publication:

Temporarily feel better about myself

XIV. What I will do if this piece is not accepted for publication:

Rework it until it is better

THE THEFT OF A KNIFE

Bartlett Adamson has made the point that Christina Handel's posthumously published novel *Not Now; I'm Not Hungry* is actually three novels. The first two sections of *Not Now; I'm Not Hungry* offer semi-autobiographical accounts of the author's own life, the first from the perspective of a spirited Canberra girl of fourteen coping with her parents' divorce, and the second from the vantage of a woman of thirty-five thrown into crisis by the unexpected reappearance of an ex-lover. The third, and shortest, part of the novel differs from these first two drastically. Titled "The Knife Takes Its First Steps Toward Manhood," it sounds many of the same notes as Jorge Luis Borges's classic short story "The South," telling the tale of a young American man who moves West with the hopes of beginning a new life. Attenuated in its syntax where Handel is usually telegraphic, sparse in its imagery where Handel is usually lush, remote from the rest of Handel's oeuvre in both its themes and its settings, this section of the novel has given critics pause since the work's publication, and most have assumed that it represented a new direction for Handel that she would have pursued had she not overdosed on a combination of barbiturates and alcohol in July 1993. Adamson, writing in the *New Australian Review* in September of that same year, is as usual an accurate barometer of the prevailing opinion: "So different is 'The Knife Takes Its First Steps Toward Manhood' from the balance of *Not Now; I'm Not Hungry*, so opposite in its method, subject, and sensibility, that we can surmise only that Handel was beginning a brave inquiry into the circularity of existence, that she was activating the political commonplace that a right-most extreme is so right-most that it becomes left-most, and activating it to ascend into new paradoxes—freedom as confinement, barbarism as civilization, youth as age, placement as displacement, and honesty as deceit."

Like all critical claims about the authorial intentions of dead writers, this assumption is thoroughly unanswerable. New evidence, however, suggests that it is also thoroughly unconvincing. Last month, a London rare-book dealer with an interest in Australian literature, and, particularly, contemporary Australian women's literature, purchased from the collector Thomas Gettelman a mothballed collection of leather-bound volumes once owned by Handel. While dusting the cover of Francis Bacon's *New Atlantis* (a book Gettelman never troubled to open), the dealer found pressed between pages a letter sent to Handel in September 1989 from an American poet named Don Herman, with whom she was romantically involved during her time in Atlanta in 1985 and 1986. In the three-page, handwritten letter, Herman asks after Handel's health, particularly her mental health—the series of nervous breakdowns that would eventually trigger her suicide had begun in the summer of 1988—and encourages her to visit him in Boston. "We can sit up late, naked, and play the summer cannibal game, laying in the cut of the sheets. We can watch the harbor through my window, which has broad brown curtains that swell grandly in the breeze. Does it appeal?"

Toward the end of the letter, Herman turns away from the personal toward the professional, noting excitedly that "I have finished another series of poems, this time mostly about silverware—as mirrors, as utensils, as anthropomorphs (who among us has not imagined himself a spoon, knife, or fork?)." "Hey, Tina," he writes in conclusion, addressing Handel by her pet name, "I have been striking some prose poses also, and have finished my story of cowboy Bruce, and how from utter hope he passes into a state of almost abject hopelessness, all as a result of a hasty judgment and an empty bag. I have enclosed this story, for your enjoyment, and as always cannot wait to hear whether it satiates or leaves you famished." In *The Collected Correspondence of Christina Handel* (University of California Press, 1995), there is no record of this letter, or any response to it, and while there are dozens of earlier letters sent from Handel to Herman and Herman to Handel, no later correspondence exists (indeed, within months it would have been impossible, since Herman died in a boating accident in January 1990). Encouraged by this recent find, librarians at the Sydney University holdings department located among another set of Handel papers a typewritten manuscript previously considered a draft of the final episode of *Not Now;*

I'm Not Hungry. The marginal handwriting on the manuscript, matching in part that of Herman's letters, suggests that this is most likely the "story of cowboy Bruce," despite the fact that the main character is named Lukke.

The question of whether Don Herman is in fact the original author of this piece, and—if so—how Herman's fiction came to be part of Handel's novel, is a perplexing one. Did Handel incorporate Herman's fiction into her own effort without his permission? Did she publish it for him as a sort of memorial tribute? Or is it possible that an overzealous publisher's assistant found the episode among Handel's papers at her death and absorbed it into the massive work-in-progress without carefully examining its provenance? Whatever the case, it seems fair to re-present "The Knife Takes Its First Steps Toward Manhood" here, with this additional bit of context restored. One final curiosity: Scholars of Handel, and in fact any careful reader familiar with *Not Now; I'm Not Hungry* will note that the final paragraph of this version of the piece differs from the version that appears in the novel. The differences are not conspicuous—they consist of two simple typographical variants in the last sentence—but they are significant, transposing concrete nouns and abstract ones and echoing the philosophical notes sounded earlier in the piece. Whether the difference between the two versions is the result of conscious alterations by Handel or another typesetter's intervention, we may never know. The fiction, however, persists on its own merits.

* * *

The young man who set out for the Six Hills Ranch in West Rock, Wyoming, in 1891 bore the name of Lukke Major, and while he was trained as an appraiser of beautiful things—of French engravings, in specific—he considered himself more of a rugged adventurer. His parents were prominent members of St. Louis's Baptist community, and left their two sons with a substantial inheritance at their death in 1890, requesting that they stay in Missouri, become doctors or clergymen. The elder brother, Marshall Major, followed the spirit of the request if not the letter, eventually gaining renown as a restaurateur across the Midwest. But Lukke Major was not particularly mindful of his heritage. Intoxicated by extravagant dreams of his own freedom, he used half of his leavings to purchase a small farm in the Wyoming plain, and spent the winter transporting himself mentally across the intervening miles. He saw the brown of the farmhouse, the gold of the surrounding fields, the cerulean blue of the Western sky, and saw in the sky what looked like angels in benevolent rotation, protecting his new farm, his grand and hopeful plan.

In St. Louis, while his brother Marshall worked as a cook and his sister Grace married an older lawyer whose garlicky mustache gainsaid an otherwise winning personality, Lukke lived a life of indolence and dissipation, drifting from woman to woman and tavern to tavern, reading Poe and the penny-sheets, telling all who would listen that the West was a lace of boundless opportunity for a man as keen and brave as he. And then, late in 1891, he set off for West Rock to claim what he had bought. He took with him very little— apart from the financial paperwork and the letter of guarantee which attested to his ownership of the ranch, both of which he kept neatly folded and filed in a leather gripsack, he carried only a few shirts, a spare pair of shoes, a philosophy primer, a black Stetson he had purchased in a haberdashery for nine dollars, and seven thousand dollars in cash. He liked to say that he valued the primer and the hat both above the cash, although this was not even close to true.

The trip from St. Louis to Wyoming began on a Monday morning. He had spent the night before in the company of cheap red wine and a young woman who was considerably more costly. Her name had been Mariana, and she claimed that she was from a good family that had fallen on bad times. "Just like the human race," Lukke had asked, laughing the bitter laugh of a man who thinks he has been granted wisdom in his youth. Lukke had been with ladies of the night before, but for some reason he was feeling especially intimate with this one, and he imagined that she was his young wife, filled with desire and hate for him, both at once. When he asked her to wear his hat, she started, and cried that she would not want to be a man, although she wouldn't say why. In the morning, Lukke took his suitcase and his gripsack (his money stacked neatly underneath his contracts and his letter of guarantee), and left.

The train station was an assembly of solitaries, the early hour demanding a personality remote from companions, a bit touched, or—in Lukke's case—an intimate of adventure. The train itself was new, and Lukke felt he was being treated to a glimpse of the future. Everything shone. Not fifteen minutes outside of St. Louis, the sight of a bird pecking at the stomach of a dead dog threw a scare into him. He wondered if it was an omen, and his optimism dimmed sharply. He consoled himself by reading Hume, and reminding himself that there was no causality but simply adjacent relations. If I push this book from my lap, he thought to himself the book falls to the ground. But I cannot say with certainty that my push causes the fall. If I scream loudly, others may come running to my aid. But I cannot say with certainty that my scream caused them to assist me. If I wait here long enough, others will enter my compartment. But I cannot say with certainty that my waiting caused the others to arrive. He entertained a seemingly endless series of false causes and effects, and at length sleep came, although he could not say with certainty that his exhaustion contributed materially.

The men who woke him came into the compartment separately, perhaps ten minutes apart, the first predictably sitting himself in the bench opposite Lukke, the second standing in the doorway and surveying the two half-occupied benches before deciding to cast his lot with the recent arrival—though he could not have known he was a recent arrival—rather than Lukke. The second man was small and burly, the first tall and lanky; both wore bowlers, and had watch fobs dangling from their vest pockets. Lukke hung on the edge of his sleep, watched the two men enter, watched them sit, watched the tall man write a letter and smoke a meerschaum pipe, and the small man file his fingernails and test his breath against a cupped palm. After the stop in Topeka, it was afternoon, shadows lengthening against the flat bright plains, and all three men relaxed enough to speak to one another. The small man introduced himself first, as Edward Brockner, an investigator for a rival railway company. He was entrusted with the safety of certain types of postal deliveries. It was all he would say about his work; "Later," he promised, "I will say more." The large man was Edward St. John, a solicitor from Boston on his way to San Francisco to oversee the establishment of a new branch of a lending institution. They spoke for a bit, Lukke explaining that he was going to the West to manage a newly acquired property and to find a wife—he had not thought about the matter of marriage before, but as he spoke it occurred to him that it was probably true. "Later," he said, "I, too, will say more." Brockner laughed, and St. John laughed too.

In the morning the fraternity of the car was upset somewhat when a woman entered and rode from Denver; she was a woman of strange appearance, unhealthily thin, with a shock of jet-black hair and a back that curved as it rose, reminding Lukke of St. Louis's wrought-iron lampposts. But her face was quite pretty, and her manner pleasant, and since Lukke felt himself to be a man of the world, a man who could speak easily to a woman of any background, he struck up a conversation with the new arrival. Brockner and St. John tucked their chins into their chests and slept. Brockner snored. The woman gave her name as Paula Ray, and said that she was a lady of the theater. "Not an actress, I'm afraid," she said. "Rather, I write."

"That's wonderful," said Lukke. "I am not often in the theater."

"All the new plays are about theft," she said. "In this they resemble the old plays."

Somewhere in the mountains, the train stopped, and

Lukke stepped out with Paula Ray, careful to take his hat and his gripsack with him. The two of them promenaded around the little town, which had a hot springs and a general store. In the store, Lukke bought himself a pipe. He didn't smoke, but he assumed he would soon begin to do so. Gallantly, he offered to make a present of a hat to Miss Ray. She accepted, and picked out a woolen cap that fit snugly atop her head. It was the same black color as her hair, and the same color as the bench near the train station where they went to sit at the conclusion of their walk. At their feet, the afternoon shadows dropped out as dusk encroached.

Feeling bold, Lukke asked Paula Ray if she had a man somewhere. "A beau," he said, when she looked confused. "Or are there many suitors?"

She stared down into the dusk. "No," she said finally. "I was married once. My husband died. I don't imagine that I will every marry again."

Lukke started to speak, but found he had nothing to say. There had been a kind of certainty in her voice that outflanked him. He just stared at the joint where her hat met her hair until the conductor called for them to board. She did not return to sit in Lukke's compartment.

* * *

Just after Salt Lake City, Brockner broke out a deck of cards and some whiskey in celebration. They played poker, and while the other men held their cards casually, Lukke kept his close to his neck, almost touching his Adam's Apple. "If the lady had stayed, we could have enjoyed a round of whist," St. John said, sniggering, and Brockner coughed into his own hand once again. Lukke was not much of a card player, but the stakes were low, pocket money only, and he quite enjoyed the camaraderie he felt with his two traveling mates, not to mention the cordial burn of Brockner's whiskey. After St. John won his third straight hand, with a queens-high full house, Brockner bore upon the others to listen to a story. "I said I would say more about my line of work," he said, "and now I mean to make good on that promise." While he was in Cincinnati, he said, he had known a man who worked for more than thirty years as a master engineer. Thirty years of distinguished service, commendations, the respect of his superiors and the adulation of those to whom he was superior. And then, one spring, he stole a knife from the foot locker of another man who was threatening to use it against a young switchman who had sassed him. The master engineer was dismissed. "He was a close acquaintance, if not exactly a friend of mine," said Brockner, "and yet I could not defend him. He had a system at his disposal, a way to report a wrongful act being plotted. Instead, he took matters into his own hands, and it was it own hands that did him in."

"Aristotle would say that the knife caused the man to steal it," Lukke said.

"What?" Brockner said. "Who's that, son?"

"Aristotle. The Greek philosopher. He thought that the plants caused the rain to fall as a way of getting nourishment."

St. John gave a rude laugh. "You should move on to more modern thinking. It's clear that the newspapers cause the rain to fall as a way of using up the space they have reserved for writing about the weather."

"I never read the newspaper," said Brockner. "In fact, I never read much of anything anymore. I once was a voracious reader, but I gave it all up after a while."

"You stopped reading?" Lukke said.

"Yes, I did," Brockner said. "At some point, it seemed to me that there was no yield in it. It wasn't that I felt that the things I was reading weren't saying anything. It's that I felt they were saying everything. One book might say that a man died when he fell from a horse. Another might say that he was crushed by his disappointment and died of a broken heart. If I do not know this man, how do I know which is true? A string of words on a piece of paper is nothing more than a lie that most men believe."

"In the law," St. John said, "it is a lie that all men believe."

Lukke ran a hand along his own leg. He was numb and more than a little drunk. He had been mumbling to himself mostly, the whiskey a somnolent trickle in his belly, and hadn't intended to speak so loudly. He sat in silence for a few minutes, and then lurched to his feet and retrieved the gripsack from the compartment overhead. "I have something to show you two fellows," he said. "You are fine fellows, and friends of mine now, so I want to show you where I am going and how I plan to make my life." He fumbled in the gripsack for the letter from the bank in West Rock. "I have a small farm that I own in Wyoming. They are expecting me. I have a guarantee." He held up the letter, which wavered in his hand. Brockner and St. John smiled at him.

Returning the letter to the gripsack, he felt around for his money, which he also wanted to show the men. It was gone. "What's the idea?" he said, taking up his hat nervously. "I had some money in here. Where has it gone?"

"How much money?" said St. John.

"Quite a bit," said Lukke. "It was an inheritance."

"Have you seen it since Salt Lake City?" Brockner asked. Lukke thought of the strange woman who had shared their compartment. A pain went through his stomach, and doubled him over.

"Let's get you to the rail detective's office," said Brockner, and Lukke took his hand. St. John steadied Lukke along his right side. His hat was in his other hand like a periapt. The two men helped him out of the car and turned toward the back of the train. Halfway down the hallway, he began to ask again about the money, louder this time. Maybe his friends would help him, go searching for the woman from car to car. Surely Brockner knew how to conduct an investigation. "Don't fall," said Brockner. "The detectives are always in the last car." St. John had him by the coat, and Lukke couldn't have fallen if he had wanted to, so tight was the man's grip on his sleeve. He held his own hat just as tightly.

Saying nothing, the men pushed Lukke into the last car, which was not an office but a baggage car. St. John kicked open a door, and the train was suddenly filled with the sound of the ground rushing by. Brockner pulled out his watch fob. At the end of the chain, there was no watch, only a flat metal rectangle that Lukke soon saw was a folding knife. With one motion, Brockner pierced Lukke's thin coat and shirt, buried the blade in the shallows of his belly, and pulled upward. With a sharp gasp, Lukke pulled the knife out and slashed at Brockner, but St. John was already upon him, choking him. Lukke dropped his hat to the floor of the car, and then was knocked down beside it by a thunderous blow from St. John. He felt at his stomach with his free hand, which came away sticky with blood, and then took his hat in his hand again. Brockner, whose face was twisted into an angry smile, threw Lukke's gripsack off—it exploded when it hit the ground, sending papers everywhere—and St. John threw Lukke off. He landed in a bed of briars, whimpering from the pain, but did not stop, simply rolled over and crawled toward the gripsack, which was wedged into underbrush near the top of a small knoll. Halfway there, a rustling noise drew his gaze downward, and there he saw his contracts for the ranch in West Rock, his dreams rendered in vellum, his future printed formally on a half-dozen envelopes. Lukke lifted one page and tried to read it, but the wind folded a corner and he could not. Replacing it on the ground, he covered it, and the others, stubbornly. They would not move now, the papers. They would never say anything other than what they said now. The ranch was his. The pain in his stomach was dull, and as small as the receding train, as he looked around him, at the knoll, and a small creek over the hill, and a redbird in a high tree branch. Not dead but maybe dying, and wondering whether he could say with any certainty that dying was a cause of death, Lukke lay there, a knife in one hand, his hate in his other, face down in the guarantee.

FRAGMENTS FROM
IVANKA! THE MUSICAL

From the first, I felt as if the fake celebrity musicals were problematic. For starters, the songs tended to be made up of many short lines in a row, and as such they wasted a tremendous amount of paper. This bothered me, and I began to leave notes all around my house reminding me to save paper. Then, Professor Onge—who confessed that he was losing sleep over the temporary delay in musical production—pointed out that the notes themselves were wastes of paper. Something in his argument was absurd, of course; something else loosed a tide of inspiration. In just a week, I was able to write "Fragments from *Napster! The Musical*," "Fragments from *The Fed! The Musical*," and "Fragments from *Salmonella! The Musical*." All were received with open arms by Professor Onge, of course, but also a public that seemingly could not get its fill of fragmentary, unperformed musicals. Below I have reprinted a representative work from that period, which has been called my glory period but which I like to remember as a period of great confusion and shame.

—B.G.

*   *   *

FRAGMENTS FROM *IVANKA! THE MUSICAL*

{PETE, a poor boy from Georgia, is preparing for the local dance contest, in which he hopes to impress the judges with his Peach Picker's Shuffle, a dance of his own invention.}

PETE:
I'm not good at making speeches.
That's not my cup of tea.
And I blush when I buckle up my breeches.
I need my privacy.
But when it comes to picking peaches
You just wait and see.

I'm a peach picker, peach picker, peach picker, peach picker.
Yeah!
Peach picker!
That's me.

{PETE goes to the barbershop to get a haircut. While there, he sees a picture of IVANKA TRUMP in a magazine. He is instantly smitten.}

PETE:
I've never heard of Thierry Mugler.
Dolce and Gabbana are all Greek to me.
Even though they sound Italian
Those fashion names just don't speak to me.

But I saw her face
In a magazine.
It's the prettiest face
That I've ever seen.

Ee-vahn-ka? Ee-vain-kah?
I wonder. I hanker
For her touch.
It's all too much.

{PETE leaves the barbershop with his hair only half-cut and boards a bus to New York City.}

PETE:
Does this bus go east?
Sir, I need to know.
Take me north, at least
Toward the ice and snow.

Does this bus go fast?
Sir, I hope it can.
I'll meet her at last.
She'll make me a man.

{PETE gets off the bus in New York City. He is immediately approached by LILY, a young prostitute who advises PETE to go to the Trump residence and wait outside for IVANKA. While he waits, he strikes up a conversation with an old doorman named WALLY. PETE tells WALLY of his plans to win IVANKA's heart.}

PETE: She's from the set that jet.
I haven't met her yet.

But I have a strong suspicion
That she'll understand my mission.

The rich, you see, are not like you and me.
They have everything but still they feel lonely.
When she finally meets my gaze it will put her in a daze.
I swear that I will be her one and only.

{PETE waits for hours but IVANKA doesn't appear. He waits the next day, and the next. Each day, he entertains WALLY with stories about Georgia. The fourth day, WALLY is not there, and PETE learns that the old man has died of a heart attack. He also discovers that WALLY's real name was really PETER EDMOND FREDRICKS, and that when he was a young man he had an obsessive love for Abby Rockefeller, the eldest daughter of John D. Rockefeller, Jr. At the time, PETER FREDRICKS was a promising young businessman, but after six months of dogged pursuit, including a sleepless week spent outside the Rockefeller residence at No. 10 W. 54th Street, he was fired from his job and was forced to become a beggar. This news fills PETE with horror. He becomes convinced that he is doomed to repeat the older PETE's fate. He takes to drink, has a brief fling with LILY, and begins talking to SPORT, a mutt he meets outside of Macy's.}

PETE:
Those shoes wouldn't fit you, old Sport.
Neither would that jacket

Or that black cotton shirt.
Why won't you speak to me, Sport?
My legs feel shaky
My heart is hurt.

{By blind luck, PETE meets IVANKA, who is coming out of her modeling agency. He falls to his knees in front of her.}

PETE:
In Georgia we were taught to do our duty
To country and to family and to God.
But no one ever taught me about beauty
When I look at you I feel kind of odd.

{Desperate to win IVANKA's love, PETE hurls himself between her and her limousine and does the Peach Picker's Shuffle. In his haste to impress her, he falls and hurts himself. From the ground, he makes one last appeal.}

PETE:
I feel like a moron.
I am sore from head to rump.
Give me your hand
So I can stand
And show you what I'm made of, good Miss Trump.

I feel like a donkey
Or a monkey on a stump.
I want one more chance.
May I have this dance

And show you what I'm made of, good Miss Trump?

{*IVANKA drives away. PETE lowers his head to the ground slowly and weeps. The ghost of WALLY/PETER FREDRICKS emerges from the clouds above, opens his mouth, but then realizes he has nothing to say.*}

THE END

IN THE PRESENCE
OF THE GENERAL

In the presence of the General, I scratch my nose. It doesn't itch, so I'm not sure why I'm doing this. Maybe I'm nervous.

The General calls the Colonel, who has a coil of rope. "Here," the General says, throwing me one end. I pull. The General pulls. We've been through this before.

Later, much later, after the pulling stops, the Colonel and I go to visit my wife, who lives in an apartment with my baby. I don't live there anymore. But we're on good terms, me and the wife and the baby. My wife is busy with a knife and some celery, but she sets her work aside and offers glasses of iced tea to me and the Colonel. He accepts, but he won't drink it. I know he won't. That guy never drinks anything, best as I can tell, or eats anything either. It's amazing that he keeps his strength. But in that rope-pulling competition, he never loses, except when he pulls against the General. You don't show up the General. The reason is rank. The reason is obvious.

My wife pours our tea, hers and mine and the Colonel's, into three identical glasses. The baby has its own glass, which is smaller and has flowers all over it and has a rubber stopper-top and is actually plastic. My wife fills that with apple juice. The baby slaps the table with open hands to show how much it wants the juice. I have also seen this baby wrap its arms around my wife's neck, and cry until its face is scarlet, and crawl across the kitchen floor. What a baby.

"So, Alice," says the Colonel, "did your husband tell you about today's tug-of-war?" He knows I haven't. We arrived together, the Colonel and I, have been in the kitchen with my wife and the baby the entire time. Telling my wife anything that the Colonel didn't hear would have been impossible, and he knows that. But the Colonel is not the kindest man, and he has always been sweet on my wife, and I think he wants to show me up in front of her.

"No, Percy," says my wife. "Am I to assume that Jim had his ass dragged across the line again?" My wife smiles when she says this. She smiles often, actually. All the time. In fact, now that I think about it, I can't honestly remember a single time I've ever seen her with any other expression on her face, even after the cancer turned up, when she was on a chemo routine so powerful it made her hair disappear entirely and then grow back in coarse, curly, and reddish. It had always been soft and brown. I moved out to live on base shortly after that. It wasn't her hair that made me go, not only, although I must admit that the last time we talked on the telephone, I imagined that her hair was brown again, and it was harder to forget about her when I put the phone down. My wife is also funny, which is a different thing than this smiling. I mean to say she tells jokes. She used to leave me little notes that had funny parts in them, like "Jim—

Went to the moon—will be back in three years. Dinner is in the freezer for you to heat. Love, Alice," when in fact she had just gone to the supermarket or the hardware store. Once at a party, one too many officers tried to buy her a drink or offer her a cigarette. "Goodness, no," she said. "I drink like a chimney and smoke like a fish." One officer laughed, either because of her smile or the joke. He had a light in his eyes the way that men sometimes do. I think it might have even been the General.

In fact, I'm sure it was the General, because later that night we got into a shoving match about it. "You were looking at her all night," I said.

"Which night?" he said. The question threw me for a second, and then he shoved me, and I shoved him back, and we went like that for a little while until the Colonel came outside to separate us. My wife was with him. "Jim," she said, "let's go home. Give me your hand." I did. "You," she said in the car on the way home. "You you you." I didn't know what she meant. That night, she spoke against the General, calling him a boor and an octopus. I found myself defending him. I spoke of his accomplishments in battle and his loyalty to his men, of his enthusiasms for new fashions and his aptitude for numbers. I explained to her why he needed to keep his nose clean. If you are a woman in the presence of the General, I remember saying, the kind of man he is needs no explanation. "I don't know what you mean," she said. I told her that it's just a fact that some women can't help but smile at men, make them feel larger and more hopeful, except for the men closest to them, who they make feel small and hopeless. Often these women smile at men in power, who then feel even more powerful. "Some women?" she said. "I could get angry, but I won't."

"What?" I say now to my wife, who is standing by the kitchen sink, emptying the Colonel's untouched glass of tea.

"What what?" she says.

"I thought I heard you call my name," I said.

"Nope," she says.

"Funny," I say. "I could swear."

"I've been sitting here the whole time," says the Colonel, "and I didn't hear anything."

"Jim," my wife says.

"What?" I say.

"What what?" she says.

"Didn't hear a thing," says the Colonel. He scratches his nose.

"Jim," my wife says.

"What?" I say. I could get angry, but I won't. We've been through this before.

"Could you bring me the baby's glass?" She is smiling broadly.

"Sure," I say. "It's right here."

I take the glass from the baby. It's empty. The baby drinks everything, and eats everything, and grabs everything. At the sink, I put the glass in the bottom of the basin, next to a knife and a half-eaten fruit I cannot immediately identify. The Colonel is telling my wife about maneuvers, and how important it is to get them right the first time. "There's no room for error," he says. "You get it wrong once, and you get it wrong forever. That's what the General always says."

"Well, he would know," my wife says. "He's quite an expert at this kind of thing. He's a prince among men. He's the guy that all the other guys want to be. Right, Jim?" I don't answer her. I brush my hand across the baby's mouth. I want the baby to smile. The baby doesn't smile. Instead, it makes a tiny fist around my index finger. The baby has a light in its eyes the way I sometimes did when I was a baby, the way I did when I was a younger man. "Right, Jim?" my wife says again. "Hey," she says. "You know what? Sometimes I get the feeling you're not listening to me." Out of the corner of my eye, I see her take the knife from the table, the one she used to cut the celery. She grasps the handle tight in her right hand, raises it over her head, and then jabs the blade toward me in short, sharp strokes. I don't turn around. I'm trying to make the baby smile. "You know I'm just joking," she says. The Colonel laughs. I can feel my wife's smile at my back. I lower my head to the baby's head, which is warm, and smells faintly of juice. I pull. The baby pulls. What a baby.

GETTING NEARER TO NEARISM

"The artist who looks too long at other artists," the essayist Pablo
Madera once wrote, "squanders the time he might spend creating,
and, diminished, becomes little more than a critic." I am fairly certain that Mr. Greenman knows of Madera's sentiments, since I
used to open each semester by reciting them—not once, not twice,
but three times. I was trying to make a distinction between inspiration and interpretation, and also to sift out those students who
would never appreciate the distinction. I was quite uncertain about
Mr. Greenman's abilities to absorb the lesson until I saw an early
draft of this work back in 1994. It has improved considerably
since—although not as much, I should say, as a work of its length
might in seven years. Madera himself, of course, was not only a
writer of essays, but also a writer of a fine piece of musical whim-
sy, which can be loosely translated as "A Dog Ate My Teeth." I do
not know if Mr. Greenman knew of this work when he began com-
posing this piece.
                                                        —L.O.

                        *   *   *

Among artists, originality and talent are prized above all
other qualities, so much so that it is rare to find a renowned
artist whose work has an absence of original vision. It is even
rarer to find a renowned artist whose work shows no sign of

artistic talent or temperament—whose work is, in a way, defiantly artless. Paolo Legno was one of those rare artists.

The Parma-born, Rome-raised Legno spent his career producing works that can broadly be classified as prints, but which are more accurately described as copies: slightly altered replicas of previously published documents. Legno's works were neither satires nor appropriations. Rather, they were exact-size imitations that differed from the originals only slightly. Legno's first works, "Menus," were near-copies of Roman restaurant menus in which he changed only the prices of the entrees, and only minimally. After "Menus," he applied the same technique to street maps, tourist pamphlets, liner notes from record albums, and advertising circulars. Over the years, Legno was called a fraud, a genius, and "a Xerox machine with an impish sense of humor"; wary of being classified with Dada, surrealism, conceptual art, or media art, Legno coined a term for his own genre, "nearism," and promptly became the world's premier nearist. One afternoon last spring, shortly after the opening of "Phone Book," a show that exhibited replicas of sections of the telephone directory, he sat down with the English painter and critic Paul Wood, a longtime friend, to discuss his career.

*   *   *

Paul Wood: Let's talk about your new work.

Paolo Legno: "White Pages" or "Yellow Pages"?

PW: Let's start with "Yellow Pages." They are a series of sheets, eight in all, that look as if they have been simply ripped out from a big-city phone book. One is taken from the Locksmith section, one from Plumbing, one from Sporting Goods: Retail, and so on.

PL: Yes.

PW: But these are not actual pages from an actual phone book.

PL: Well, they are partly actual. In "Air Conditioning: Repair," for example, I only altered the names of four repair companies and then the phone numbers of four different companies. I left the layout of the page, and the artwork, exactly as it was in the original version.

PW: So if I were to call these phone numbers, I would not reach air conditioning repairmen?

PL: You might. Remember, I did not change them all. It is possible that you might select one in which the name and the number are as they were in the original.

PW: Tell me a little bit about your process. Do you create these by hand?

PL: I use the same process as the people who created the originals. I design the files in a desktop publishing program, and then I output them to the same kind of paper. In the case of "Yellow Pages," I used the same commercial printer.

PW: So how are your works different than the originals?

PL: Slightly. And at the same time, entirely.

PW: What is the point of this exercise? Is it like Borges's Pierre Menard, who exactly rewrote sections of Cervantes's *Don Quixote*?

PL: No. It's not, really. Menard is an interesting case, but not the same case as me, because the original *Quixote* required an astounding amount of creative energy, and the second *Quixote* required considerably less. I use originals that required little or no creative energy, and I expend some creative energy in copying them, in that I must invent new names or words or numbers. Borges is writing about a man who is, arguably, less creative than his sources. I am, inarguably, more creative than mine. Should that not give me some measure of satisfaction?

PW: You have said that you are simply making explicit the debts that are implicit in every artwork.

PL: Every artist has sources. Picasso drew on African art. Rauschenberg looked at Johns. When I first started my career as an artist, I was a painter, and I was utterly indebted to Hockney, enslaved to painting works that had a brilliance of hue that concealed the banality of their subject. It was difficult to liberate myself from that. It took great effort, and almost cost me my creative life. Having unshackled myself, I was free to do whatever I wanted.

PW: But drawing stylistic inspiration from another piece of art is somewhat different than borrowing large amounts of another piece of non-artistic printing.

PL: The cardinal rule of this sort of thing is that the cardinal rule is an ordinal rule. What is first is first. Everything else is not-first: Second, third, fourth, these are secondary distinctions, but not-first is the primary one. We have the original, and we have the others.

PW: You could say that about any artistic representation. We have life, and then we have art. We have fact, and then we have fiction.

PL: Yes. But I like to think of my work as fact.

PW: Well, even nonfiction is a representation of sorts. That's why we have literary nonfiction.

PL. Not literary nonfiction, though. Fact. As far as I am concerned, my works are entirely factual.

PW: Meaning that they are entirely true? But you know that they are not true, because you have changed information. The price of an item according to one of your "Grocery Store Specials" is not actually the price. The time a movie is showing according to one of your "Movie Times" is not actually the time. You know that because you have read the actual information, and then changed it.

PL: Is a fact that which is indisputably true or is a fact that which assumes the stance of truthfulness?

PW: Is that a rhetorical question?

PL: No.

PW: Okay. Let's talk about counterfeiting. Do you consider yourself a kind of counterfeiter or forger?

PL: I suppose so. But the great forgers work hard to mimic the style of the works they are copying, whether it's currency or Matisse. I do not work hard. It is easy. Because the work is without style. No, that's not right: not without style, but without difficult style. It has an easy style: a certain kind of paper, a certain font, a certain piece of clip art. Simple colors. Simple arrangement. This is what I was saying before about the relative difficulty of these works. It is much more difficult to forge the "Mona Lisa" than to forge a poster promising specials on Granny Smith apples. The "Mona Lisa" forger might give himself away by not exactly capturing the eye of the original. I could create a verisimilar poster with ease, but I choose to change it slightly: maybe these apples are 99¢ per pound rather than $1.09 per pound.

PW: Does your work, after it is created, become its own original?

PL: Of course. And I will tell you something. I had a student a few years ago who decided to make artworks that stood in relation to my works as my works stand in relation to, say, the public telephone directory, or the newspaper ads. He took my work and he created his own electronic file, and he changed a few more things, and he printed them, and he showed them as his own.

PW: Did he get an A?

PL: He did. He was a clever student. But he started me thinking about this, and since then, I have been working on my own second-generation works, in which I work off of my own copies and change the information again.

PW: So you have a work that is even more distant from the original?

PL: That's what is interesting. The second set of changes has, for some reason, been exactly counterweighting the first set of changes. So the second-generation copy ends up being exactly the same as the original.

PW: So will these be your next works?

PL: I am thinking about exhibiting my second-generation copies alongside the orignals. They are distant cousins who are also identical twins. The slight alteration of my slight alteration is myself. Or else I may exhibit a different set of pieces that I have recently begun. They are catalogs from past shows, and I have collected them, and reprinted them.

I am thinking about binding them into a book.

PW: And they just have a few details changed?

PL: No. When it came to the catalogs, I changed almost everything. It is the incontinent version of the controlled experiment I have been performing for the last decade, and it is an exciting departure. I tell you, it is incredibly liberating to be able to change your name, the titles of your works, the dimensions of them, everything but the pictures. I have recreated a version of my restaurant menus where the works exhibited are, according to the notation in the catalog, twenty feet tall. Can you imagine these monumental menus? You would need a waiter more than a hundred feet tall just to carry them to your table.

. . .

Soon after the opening of "White Pages/Yellow Pages," Madera invited Legno to speak at a symposium in Barcelona. Legno agreed. When he did not appear as scheduled and would not answer his phone, Wood had police enter Legno's hotel room. They found the artist in his bathroom, dead by his own hand. "Those who take their own lives," he once wrote in a letter to the Polish critic Inek Drzewo, "should go by pills, because pills are painless and free of mess, and because they have a printed label that lends itself quite nicely to nearism in a way that other instruments of oblivion, whether gun, rope, or automobile, do not." Legno was perverse even in death. He did not use pills, but rather a pistol, and the fatal course he plotted was hardly free of mess—the officer who discovered his body said that the scene was "like a painting made with blood." To the pistol, Legno had taped a small label on which he had typed the word "gun."

TEN KINDS OF THINGS, A–H

1. Things that I have thought about recently
2. Things that I haven't thought about in a long time
3. Things that have proud histories
4. Things that I have eaten or considered eating
5. Things that are easy to overlook
6. Things that I have given away
7. Things that cause happiness
8. Things that cause frustration
9. Things that have no smell
10. Things that are in my pocket right now

* * *

5-ACCORDION
1-ACETONE
4-ACID
2-ADAPTOR, ELECTRICAL
4-ADHESIVE TAPE
4-ADVERTISING CIRCULAR & FLIERS

5-AEROGRAMME, UNUSED

1-AEROSOL

3-ALARM CLOCK

5-ANSWERING MACHINE

4-ANTS

1-APPLE PITS

4-APRICOT PIT

2-AQUARIUM, EMPTY

7-AQUARIUM, WITH FISH

4-ARTICHOKE, RAW

5-ARTICLE FOR SALE

2-ASHTRAY

4-ASPARAGUS, RAW

1-ASTRONOMY BOOKS

2-AUTOMOBILE

3-AUTOMOBILE, PARKED IN FRONT OF HOUSE

4-AVOCADO PEEL & PIT

6-BABY CARRIAGE, WITH WHEEL FALLEN OFF

1-BAG OF SUGAR

2-BAKER'S SHOVEL

4-BAKING POWDER

2-BAKING TIN

1-BALL

4-BALL-COCK IN WATERTANK

1-BALLOON, DEFLATED

4-BANANA, GREEN (INEDIBLE)

1-BANDAGE

4-BARLEY, UNCOOKED

5-BAROMETER

1-BASEBALL EQUIPMENT

1-BASKETBALL

1-BATH CURTAIN

3-BATTERY

1-BATTERY CLOCK

4-BED PAN

2-BELL

4-BICARBONATE OF SODA

5-BICYCLE

1-BINOCULARS

7-BIRDCAGE, WITH BIRD

2-BIRDCAGE, EMPTY

5-BIRTH CERIFICATE

4-BLACK-EYED PEA, RAW

3-BLACKBOARD

1-BLEACH

5-BLOOD PRESSURE TESTER

5-BLUEPRINTS

2-BOARD GAMES

1-BOAT

9-BONES

1-BOOKS

1-BOOTS

1-BOTTLE OPENER

1-BOTTLE, WITH SCREW-ON CAP

1-BRAN

3-BROKEN DISHES

1-BROOM, SOFT

6-BROOM, WITHOUT HANDLE

1-BRUSH, FOR BABY BOTTLES

2-BRUSH, HAIR (HARD BRUSH)

1-BRUSH, HAIR (SOFT BRUSH)
1-BRUSH, HOUSEHOLD
1-BRUSH, FOR WASHING DISHES
2-BRUSH, FOR WASHING FLOOR
1-BUILDING BLOCKS, CHILDREN'S
5-BULB, ELECTRIC
4-BUS TICKET
8-BUTTON
4-CACTUS PEAR, PEEL
4-CAKE MIXES
5-CALCULATOR
5-CAMERA
4-CAMPHOR
2-CAN, EMPTY
8-CANDELABRA
3-CANDLE, WAX
7-CANDLESTICKS
4-CANDY WRAPPER
1-CANNED GOODS
2-CAR
3-CARBON PAPER
4-CAROB, PITS
6-CARPET
2-CARPET BEATER
1-CARROT, PEEL
2-CASSETTES
4-CASTOR OIL
2-CATALOGS
2-CAT BED
1-CAULIFLOWER

1-CHAIR, DIRT & DUST ON

3-CHALK

5-CHANDELIER

4-CHAPSTICK

1-CHECKERS

4-CHERRY, PITS

1-CHESS

5-CHECKS

1-CHILDREN'S CAR

3-CIGARETTE

2-CIGARETTE, CASE

3-CIGARETTE, LIGHTER

3-CIGARETTE, PACK

4-CINDER BLOCKS

1-CITRIC ACID

4-CLAY

1-CLEANING CLOTH

4-CLEMENTINE

1-CLOCK, ELECTRIC

1-CLOCK, HANDS OF

1-CLOCK, KNOBS OF

4-CLOCK, STOPPED OR BROKEN

5-CLOCK, WALL

2-CLOCK, WIND UP KEY

4-COCKROACH

1-COCOA

4-COCONUT, SHELL

1-COCONUT, GROUND

4-COFFEE BEANS

1-COFFEE, INSTANT

10-COINS

1-COLORING BOOK

10-COMB

1-COMBINATION LOCK

5-CONSTRUCTION PAPER

1-CONTAINER, YOGURT

5-CONTRACTS

8-CORD USED AS ELECTRIC SWITCH

1-CORKSCREW

4-CORN FLOUR

6-CORN ON THE COB, RAW

4-COSMETICS, CREAM FORM

4-COTTON SEEDS

2-COUNTER-TOP APPLIANCES

9-COVER OF UNDERGROUND ELECTRICITY BOX

2-CRYSTAL ASHTRAY

1-CRYSTAL WARE

1-CUCUMBER, PEEL

4-DATE PIT

4-DENTAL FLOSS

4-DEODORANT STICK

4-DETERGENT

2-DIAPER, CLEAN

4-DIAPER, DIRTY

1-DIGITAL WATCH

1-DIRT ON FLOOR

2-DOG BED

1-DOLLS THAT TALK

1-DOOR KNOCKER

5-DRILL, ELECTRIC

5-DRIVER'S LICENSE

2-DRUM, CHILDREN'S

5-DRYER

2-DRYER, DOOR

1-DUST PAN

1-DUSTER

4-DOUGH

3-DOUGH HOOK

1-EAR PLUG, RUBBER

3-EAR PLUG, WAX

10-EGG LAID ON SHABBOS

1-EGG, RAW

4-EGG, SHELL

4-EGGPLANT, RAW

1-EGG SLICER

1-EGG WITH BLOOD

2-ELECTRIC BLANKET

5-ELECTRIC LIGHT

5-ELECTRIC MIXER

8-ELECTRIC SWITCH

1-ELECTRIC SWITCH, COVER OVER

5-ENVELOPE

3-ERASER

2-ERECTOR SET

1-EXTRACTS, BAKING

4-EYE COLOR

2-FAN

4-FAUCET, FALLEN OFF

1-FAUCET ON WATER TANK

1-FEATHER ON GARMENT

4-FERTILIZER

3-FEVER TESTER

5-FILM, PHOTOGRAPHIC

1-FILTER, TAP

5-FIRE EXTINGUISHER

4-FISH, LIVE

1-FISHFOOD

5-FLASH BULB

2-FLASHLIGHT

1-FLAVORING

4-FLIES

2-FLIPPERS

4-FLOOR CLEANER (LIQUID)

1-FLOOR RAG

3-FLOOR RAG (DAMP)

6-FLOOR RAG (VERY WET)

4-FLOUR

2-FLOUR SIFTER

1-FLOWERS

1-FLOWERS, ARTIFICIAL

1-FLOWERS, IN VASE

5-FLUORESCENT LAMP

2-FLUTE

2-FLY SWATTER

1-FOOD FOR SALE

1-FOOTBALL

1-FOOTBALL, DEFLATED

5-FRAGILE ARTICLES

1-FROZEN FOOD

4- FRUIT, UNRIPE

2-FRYING PAN
2-FUNNEL, WITH SIEVE
1-GARBAGE BAG
1-GARBAGE CAN, EMPTY
2-GARDENING TOOLS
4-GARLIC, PEEL
1-GARLIC POWDER
1-GARLIC SALT
5-GAS, BURNER
1-GAS, COVER OVER STOVE
3-GAS, CYLINDER TANK
4-GASOLINE
4-GAS PIPE
5-GAS STOVE
1-GAUZE PADS
3-GIFT, UNGIVEN
4-GIFT, GIVEN
1-GINGER, GROUND
4-GINGER, UNGROUND
1-GLASS, BROKEN
9-GLASSES, BROKEN
4-GLASSES, FRAME BROKEN
7-GLASSES, LENS BROKEN
3-GLASSES, LENS LOST
2-GLASSES, SCREW FELL OUT
1-GLOVES, RUBBER
4-GLUE
4-GOLDFISH
1-GOURD, RAW
4-GRAIN

1-GRAPEFRUIT, PEEL & PITS

1-GRAPE, PITS

4-GRASS

2-GRATER

4-GREEN PEPPER, SEEDS

2-GRINDER, FOOD

2-GRINDSTONE

1-GUARDRAIL, PORTABLE

1-GUAVA, PEELS & PITS

5-GUITAR

1-HAND CLEANER

4-HAND CREAM

2-HAMMER

4-HANDLE OF DOOR (BROKEN)

2-HARMONICA

7-HEARING AID

2-HEATER, ELECTRIC

7-HERBAL TEA

2-HOLE PUNCHER

4-HOOK, WITH SCREW

4-HOOK, WITH SUCTION CUP

4-HOOK & EYE

1-HORSERADISH

1-HOT PEPPER

1-HOT-WATER BOTTLE

3-HUMIDIFIER

4-HUNTING KNIFE

FRAGMENTS FROM
DYLAN! THE VARIETY SHOW

In the spring of 2000, the legendary musician Bob Dylan signed a deal with the cable network Home Box Office in which the two parties agreed that the first party, Mr. Dylan, would star in a one-hour TV variety show broadcast by the second party, Home Box Office. The special would be created especially for Mr. Dylan by the writer and producer Larry Charles, who earlier earned fame as a co-creator of *Seinfeld* and *Mad About You*, both of which were popular sitcoms in the nineteen-nineties. Both Home Box Office and Mr. Dylan were tight-lipped about the program. Only Larry Charles spoke, and he promised that the show would be "unpredictable, unsettling, distinctive, original, and entertaining, all at the same time."

At the same time, my certainty that the fake celebrity musical format had run its course was greater than ever. The musicals suddenly seemed like strange creatures to me: petty, pointless, and doomed to extinction. What was the justification for "Fragments from *Major Indoor Soccer League! The Musical*"? "Levity, of course, where gravity fails you," Professor Onge wrote, but I disagreed. A fake celebrity variety show, on the other hand, seemed like it could really take off. I rubbed my hands together with glee.

—*B.G.*

*   *   *

103

FRAGMENTS FROM *DYLAN!* *THE VARIETY SHOW*

{Fade in: Suburban home, interior. TIM CONWAY is standing by the widow.}

TIM CONWAY: It's such a nice afternoon; I think I'll just go sit in my easy chair and read a magazine.

{Doorbell rings}

TIM CONWAY: Who is it?

{Opens door to reveal BOB DYLAN in mailman's costume}

TIM CONWAY: Oh, it's the mailman. Do you have a package for me?

DYLAN: *{unintelligible}*

TIM CONWAY: Uh-huh.

DYLAN: *{unintelligible}*

TIM CONWAY: I understand.

DYLAN: *{unintelligible}*

TIM CONWAY: Yes, of course.

DYLAN: *{unintelligible}*

TIM CONWAY: But I don't own a duck!

{HARVEY KORMAN enters, carrying duck.}

DYLAN: *{unintelligible}*

TIM CONWAY: I have never seen this man before!

DUCK: I'm not a man, I'm a duck.

DYLAN: *{unintelligible}*

{Fade out}

* * *

{Fade in: Office decorated with Jewish artifacts. ELI WAL-LACH, dressed as a rabbi, is addressing BEN STILLER, JON STEWART, and JERRY SEINFELD.}

ELI WALLACH: You have reached your final exams to become rabbis. I want you to understand, though, that being a rabbi isn't only about leading a prayer service. It's about counseling the members of your congregation. Do all of you understand that?

BEN STILLER: Yes.

JON STEWART: Yes.

JERRY SEINFELD: I think I understand.

ELI WALLACH: Okay. As part of today's final exam, we're going to bring in Mr. Silverstein. He has a problem that he'll explain.

{DYLAN enters}

DYLAN: *{unintelligible}*

{The three junior rabbis stare in open-mouth silence.}

BEN STILLER: Uh...

JERRY SEINFELD: Er...

JON STEWART: How does a 60-year-old man even get a Pokémon water pistol, let alone get it stuck up there?

DYLAN: *{unintelligible}*

{fade out}

* * *

{Fade in. LILY TOMLIN stands on darkened stage.}

LILY TOMLIN: Hello, I'm Lily Tomlin. Abbie Hoffman once said, "Don't trust anyone over thirty." But now, everyone he said it to is over thirty, and the sixties are just a chapter in the history books. That doesn't mean, though, that we can't recapture that time through our friendships, our memories, and—most importantly—high-priced collectibles designed to capitalize on our nostalgia. Over the last decade, the Frumpkin Mint has offered everything from Beatles collectible coins to Jefferson Airplane plates to the Altamont commemorative pocketknife. Now, though, we have done ourselves one better. We are pleased to announce that we are making available, for the first time anywhere, Bob Dylan. Not Bob Dylan stamps. Not Bob Dylan thimbles. No: Bob Dylan himself.

{Lights in back of LILY TOMLIN go up to reveal DYLAN.}

LILY TOMLIN: For years, Dylan has been one of the most important symbols of the nineteen-sixties, both for his political consciousness and for his poetic songs. And now, you can own him. For a reasonable initial cost of $99.95, and five monthly installments of $39.95, Dylan can be yours and yours alone. This is a unique offer, exclusive to Frumpkin Mint customers and not available anywhere else in the world. Just think of how much joy Dylan will bring into your life. Interested in hearing "The Times They Are A-Changing"? Don't bother digging through your old record crates. Just tell Dylan to sing you a verse.

DYLAN: Come mothers and fathers, throughout the land. And don't criticize what you can't understand.

LILY TOMLIN: Or maybe you'd like to recreate one of his combative, maundering mid-sixties interviews. *{turns to DYLAN}* Mr. Dylan, have you stopped writing protest songs?

DYLAN: Well, you know, "against" and "for" are just words, man, and I'm not going to be the one to say them. My songs are constructed from pieces of thoughts and strung together with numbers, so I'm not going to say any more than that. If you listen specifically, you'll hear that there's a Spanish thing, and then a Chinese thing, and then you'll have plenty of time to see what I mean.

LILY TOMLIN: Dylan can even personalize some of his greatest songs, especially for you.

DYLAN: The answer, my friend Lily, is blowing in the wind.

LILY TOMLIN: If you're not entirely satisfied, you can return your purchase within thirty days. Order now and receive, at no additional cost, Donovan.

{Fade out}

* * *

{Fade in}

{DYLAN appears on a raised pedestal, around which are two dozen young men and women dressed in black-and-white bodysuits. When he begins to sing "Rainy Day Women #12 & 35," the dancers stagger around the stage, pretending to smoke marijuana and drink alcohol. Then he switches to "Like a Rolling Stone," and the male dancers ball up and tumble across the stage while the female dancers look around in confusion, as if they have no direction home. Next is "I Shall Be Released," during which the female

dancers embrace the male dancers and then — after squinting into the distance as if looking at the sunset — release them. Dylan concludes with "Tangled Up In Blue," a big production number in which blue streamers fall from the ceiling and all the dancers wrap themselves in the streamers and twist from side to side.}

{Fade out}

*   *   *

{fade in. DYLAN stands on darkened stage.}
DYLAN: *{unintelligible}*
{DYLAN waves goodnight.}

NOTES TO A PAPER YOU WOULDN'T UNDERSTAND

1. In the fifties, Vinton was still entirely defined by his association with the Enjoin movement: see Randolph Descombes, "The Enjoin Poets Make Less with More Language"; Francis Embry, "What Goes Down Must Come Up"; and a volume jointly edited by Descombes and Embry entitled *Desire Cannot Be Contained*. The last of these is of special interest, since it contains the essay in which Umberto Gettlioni suggested that Vinton try his hand at writing prose. "There is one among them," he wrote, "who has thus far labored, in my mind, in the wrong mine. I mean, of course, George Vinton, whose work has shown the least promise of any of the first wave of Enjoin poets. Vinton's problem, I believe, is not one of incompetence, but rather of dislocation. Were he to write a series of short stories or a novel, I feel we might see a different man."(99) Kenneth Burnham was shown the essay by Michelangelo Gettlioni, Umberto's nephew, and mentioned it to Vinton in a letter. "Dear boy," he wrote, "some addlepated critic has come up with a preposterous notion that your talents should be wasted telling stories."

2. Weeks before his first motorcycle accident, Vinton had what he called an "insultingly, transparently prophetic dream." In a journal entry of June 8, 1958, he wrote, "Motorcycle crashing. Could not see face of man riding cycle, but believe that it was me from name tag on jacket that read 'G. Vinton.'" The journal entry is also noteworthy in that it contains the first mention of Lynn Short, who was introduced to Vinton at a party and stuck in his mind as a result of her "red hair and shoes."

3. "Touch, tip, shatter, repair, touch, tip, shatter, repair, touch, tip, shatter, repair, touch, tip, shatter, repair. It's a beautiful line, granted, but now I'm out four vases." (11) Vinton's "What Is Left of Her Lips" was published in a chapbook edition of two hundred in June of that year, and Burnham, the unofficial leader of the Enjoin movement, immediately hailed it as a masterpiece.

4. Zeno's Paradox, of course, is the age-old mathematical/philosophical conundrum that holds that it is impossible to travel from Point A to Point B, because travel can be expressed as a infinite series of halvings of the interval distance. Xeno's Paradox, less well known, was posed by the early twentieth-century British writer, Geoffrey Stanhope, who adopted the Greek nom de plume as a tribute to his forbears, and it concerns the problem of artistic representation. "Is a picture more or less real than the object it depicts?" Stanhope wrote. "If a dying man sits for a portrait, and then expires, and his picture persists, who is to say that it is not more real than the man, or more real

than he had ever been?" Vinton recommended Stanhope's work to Lynn Short, and during a vacation they took to Capri in 1961, he gave her a copy. In return, she gave Vinton a copy of Hammett's "The Continental Op," a decision, of course, that proved immensely influential.

5. Burnham's behavior was archetypal in this regard, and when he felt that he was losing Vinton to Short, he immediately sought out the company of the critic Howard Salter, a man to whom he bore an uncanny physical resemblance. See V. Petrancko, "Mentorship as a Form of Displaced Narcissism" (Chicago, 1974) for a full account of the symptoms.

6. Few have remarked upon the fact that it was his second visit to Brisbane. The first, five years earlier, had been in the company of Burnham, and it was under the older man's influence that Vinton wrote the vast majority of "A Grand and Hopeful Plan." With Short, Vinton sketched out the plot for his first mystery novel, *The Damned Shame of Louis Soule*. Burnham was heartbroken when he heard of Vinton's plans: "There is no pain sharper than this news," he wrote.

7. Some critics have even suggested that Mark Petty's name is a pun of sorts, Vinton's attempt to encode his equivocal feelings about the written word. Lance Warner's "Evasive Action" is a good general study of what he calls "self-seditious texts," Vinton's among them. See also A. Childs, "When Is a Whodunit Not a Whodunit? Solving the Puzzle of Plotlessness in the Mystery Novels of George Vinton."

8. "Need title for new book," he wrote to Short as he labored to produce a sequel to *The Damned Shame of Louis Soule.* "Working title is 'Working Title,' but I'm not happy with this. Also considering 'Not Happy with This,' which seems slightly better." Vinton also considered a series of radical stylistic experiments, at one point telling an interviewer that he planned to write an extremely short mystery, all of which would be printed on the cover of the book, and that the pages inside would be blank.

9. John Preston's "Detectives and Retextualization" and Frances Gay's "Planted Clues" both examine the role of obsessive behavior in Vinton's mystery novels. Preston proposes that detection is itself a form of compulsion, while Gay looks at the way in which Vinton concerns himself with the role of lists.

10. Though *The Raw Deal of Walter Brown* would prove to be even more successful than *The Lost Cause of Arthur Cross.* Vinton had great doubts about the work. In fact, he wrote Burnham a letter listing nineteen reasons why he feared the book would be a failure, including "Because readers will not see that the mystery is constructed with perfect symmetry," "Because readers will be displeased by the seemingly random relationship between short chapters and long chapters," and "Because Mark Petty never does anything. Sits, thinks, sits thinks, sits." "Still," he wrote, "there is an answer, and it sits at the dead center of the novel, and I believe that those who find it deserve their reward entirely."

11. It is unquestionable that Howard Salter's famous critique of *The Raw Deal of Walter Brown* incorporated the material from Vinton's letter to Burnham. Vinton, who had not known about the relationship between Salter and Burnham—the former was a married man who did not admit his homosexuality until 1973—was perplexed at first, and then furious. "I wish I had sent you a puffed-up, preening, bit of self-congratulatory nonsense," he wrote. "Then maybe Salter would have written a good review. He does not seem to think for himself."

12. A similar thesis has been developed by L.T. Honegger: see *The Locus of Location: A Brief Consideration of the Topographical Psychology ("Boekbesprekingen") of Anthropomor-phism.*

13 . The most flagrant of the psychoanalytic critics is indisputably Marjorie Leacock: "Burnham was clearly ashamed of Salter, but was also angry at Vinton for what he perceived as a betrayal. Consider the letter of July 9, 1968, in which Burnham attempts to make Vinton feel guilty by relating a story about how he came to break a finger while reaching for a book of Vinton's. The tropes of emasculation, impotence, betrayal, and intimacy are so clear they might as well be in a textbook."

14. This was never published, despite Burnham's threats. Instead, Burnham began to refer to Short as "my daughter-in-law" and to Vinton as "my estranged son." After the birth of Vinton and Short's first child, Louis Walter Vinton, Burnham gave an interview to the Kansas City *Star* in

which he complained that he was being "denied the right to see my grandson."

15. It was this phone call that led Vinton to write the famous closing lines of *The Rotten Luck of Marvin Eagleton*: "He picked up the dead man's hand and looked at it for a while. It was a hand like any other hand, and as such did not hold his interest long."

16. Vinton's interest in libraries as sites of crimes is one of the most studied aspects of his oeuvre. See Nicholas Prince, *Metareference in the Library of the Mind,* and Albert Haake, *Speaking Volumes*.

17. There is no doubt that *The Troubled Mind of Fredrick Furst* was intended as an attack against Burnham. The victim, Fredrick Furst, is an aging gay painter who is murdered by a young man who is in the process of rejecting his advances.

18. John Tock's "Doing Time" is an excellent study of the use of prolepsis in Vinton's mysteries.

19. Burnham's death was ruled an accident, although Salter believed otherwise, and said so in a letter to Vinton that he composed but never mailed. It is now part of the Howard Salter Papers at the University of Texas. "Ask anyone who knew him," Salter wrote. "To say that you betrayed him is something of an understatement. Worst of it is that he never meant to hurt you. Ken Burnham was a good man who

loved your poems, and who felt that your other work was beneath you. He was honor-bound to say so, and you, my boy, were honor-bound to listen. You did not. You mocked. You lampooned. And in the end, you murdered him with your words. You cannot say that Ken was a villain. At worst, you can accuse him of being a critic; as one myself, I know the full horror of that existence."

FRAGMENTS FROM *ELIAN!*
THE MUSICAL

For a time, I gave no thought to fake celebrity musicals. I learned to swim, and to read, and to make those paper-plate-and-dried-bean shakers that can be used as primitive percussion instruments. My life was, if not happy, at least blissful. But then a young Cuban boy named Elian Gonzalez decided to be born to a mother who resolved, somewhat crazily, to take him from Havana to Miami on a raft. Elian's mother, of course, died. Her son survived to become the focus of an international incident. Everything about the Elian story screamed "fake celebrity musical." Then Professor Onge screamed "fake celebrity musical." He was on the telephone, which I knew I should not have answered. I know that I had vowed never to serve that muse again, but it was as if my resolve were made of eggs and the Elian situation broke that resolve and made an omelet of it. And that omelet must have smelled good to someone: in the weeks following the publication of this musical, at least two insistent theatrical producers contacted me about bringing it to the stage, and extremely similar musicals appeared in *The Washington Post* and on the television series *Saturday Night Live*. None of this, however, lessened my distaste for fake celebrity musicals. Professor Onge was jubilant. I was miserable. Together, you might say, we were juberable.   —*B.G.*

FRAGMENTS FROM *ELIAN! THE MUSICAL*

{The adult ELIAN GONZALES (Freddie Prinze, Jr.) is watching children playing soccer in a field. When a ball is kicked toward him, ELIAN retrieves it and begins to sing.}

ADULT ELIAN:
Out of bounds
I know just how this soccer ball must feel.
Kicked around
My own life to me sometimes seems unreal.
Mi vida was loca.
One day I awoke-a
To find my mother standing with a smile.
Get dressed, she said.
Get out of bed.
We're going to Miami for a while.

{Flashback: A boat, at sea, is trapped in the middle of a storm. The young ELIAN (Jonathan Lipnicki, hair dyed black) is holding tight to his MOTHER (Jennifer Lopez).}

ELIAN:
Mama! Mama!
Don't fall into the sea.
For if you fall
I am so small
What will become
Of me?

MOTHER:
Don't forget
Mi hijo
America is over there.
And in America
You'll have good food to eat
And shirts that you don't have to share
And tennis shoes with pumps in them
That fill the soles with air!

{The boat capsizes, drowning ELIAN's MOTHER and many of the other passengers. ELIAN finds an inner tube and holds on for dear life. Two days later, he washes up on the shores of Miami. American relatives claim him, and he becomes the focus of an international dispute when Cuban dictator FIDEL CASTRO (Mandy Patinkin) demands his return.}

FIDEL CASTRO:
In the matter of Gonzales
Take a letter
Or should I say dictation?
It wasn't just by accident
That I rose to lead this nation.
Don't mess with me
I beat Batista.
I'll have him back here
Before Easter
A holiday that we don't celebrate.
I'm sure the decadent Americans
Are letting that boy stay up way too late.

{In Miami, the Cuban community, and then the entire city, erupts into divisive debate. Two elderly men, MILTON (Walter Matthau) and GEORGE (Jack Lemmon) argue the two sides of the issue.}

MILTON:
The truth is plain to see
If he's not here, he's gone
You left-wing fool!
You'd have him be
A Communistic pawn.

GEORGE:
The boy should be sent home.
He has a father there
You right-wing fool!
You own a comb
But not a strand of hair!

{Back in Cuba, ELIAN's FATHER (Andy Garcia) laments his son's absence.}

FATHER:
It's driving me bananas
To wait here in Havana
For my boy.
I've lost him to the land
Of New York and the Rio Grande
Hollywood and Maine and Illinois.

119

Though I'm somewhat outspoken
I'm no politician.
I sit on no commission.
It would take a real magician
To fix what has been broken.
It would take a David Copperfield
Or even Sigfried and/or Roy
To make sure that my wound is healed
And bring me back my boy!

{In the wake of Congressional hearings on ELIAN, intensifying protests, and rumors that ELIAN is growing accustomed to his new life in America, his two grandmothers, RAQUEL RODRIGUEZ (Olympia Dukakis) and MARIELA QUINTANA (Lauren Bacall), come to Washington to plead for their grandson's return.}

GRANDMOTHERS:
He's just a little child
What on earth does he know?
The winds of change blow wild
Look! Here comes Janet Reno

{JANET RENO (Sigourney Weaver) meets with the two grandmothers. Congress meets with the two grandmothers. JANET RENO meets with Congress. The two grandmothers meet with ELIAN. Then the two grandmothers, confused, meet with each other. Finally, ELIAN steps into the spotlight.}

ELIAN:
Wait!

Why will no one ask me what I think?
Wait!
This idiotic crisis has pushed me to the brink

{He is joined onstage by the adult ELIAN, still holding the soccer ball.}

ADULT ELIAN:
What's that?
A voice.
What is
His choice?

ELIAN:
Wait!
Please let me express my own opinion.
Wait!
When it comes to my own fate, I must have dominion.

ADULT ELIAN:
His shiny eyes
His ruddy cheeks
The political football speaks.
He speaks.

ELIAN:
Wait!
I demand to be heard.
Wait!
Just one lousy word.

{The curtains part to show the entire cast, including FIDEL CASTRO, MILTON, GEORGE, JANET RENO, ELIAN's FATHER, and the ghost of ELIAN's mother. As they sing, the adult Elian holds the soccer ball aloft.}

ALL:
The ocean is wide
As wide as an ocean
As wide as this little boy's
Innermost emotions.
So go now, boy,
And kick this ball into the goal
And know now, boy,
That the truest freedom
Is the freedom of the soul.
That's right: the truest freedom
Is the freedom of the soul!

{The young Elian storms off, disgusted.}

BLURBS

"Devilishly brilliant—a bewitching mix of metafiction and marketing."

—*The New York Times*

"In just four-hundred words, this piece dismantles the history of modern literature and pieces it back together again."

—*The Los Angeles Times*

"The central conceit—a humor piece composed entirely of blurbs about that humor piece—reads like a Mobius strip tied around Jorge Luis Borges's finger."

—*The Boston Globe*

"Every writer dreams of writing his own blurbs. This writer has done that, and only that, and benefitted immensely from it. His sly wit conceals a grand scheme, and the completion of that scheme only intensifies the power of that wit."

—*The Washington Post*

"After the first blurb, you'll find yourself confused. After the second, amused. But by the fourth or fifth, you'll find yourself cheering."

—*USA Today*

"Initial bemusement will turn to wonder—this is sophisticated stuff indeed."

—*Kirkus Reviews*

"Imagine a cross between the blurbs from *Bridges of Madison County* and the blurbs from *Infinite Jest*."

—*The Cleveland Plain Dealer*

"Marvelous . . . Bracing . . . A short, sharp work combining myth and romance, social commentary and poetry."

—*Publishers Weekly*

"'Blurbs' has the advantage of novelty, but it is not simply a novelty. Rather, it is something startling, an entirely new foray into our critical assumptions about literature, both high and low."

—*The Houston Chronicle*

"A splendid piece, beautifully conceived and crafted ... No other collection of blurbs this year comes close."

—*The San Jose Mercury News*

"If John Barth met Samuel Beckett in a bar, and the two of them got into a cab, and the cab picked up Andy Kaufman, and then the cab driver turned around, and it was Dorothy

Parker, that would be awfully strange. It would also be the rough equivalent of this marvelous short work."

—*The Baltimore Sun*

"In the traditional humor piece, society is satirized with the help of plot, or characters. 'Blurbs' throws that all away, bravely, and what it finds is something much more precious: a purity of comic conception that holds a mirror up to the entire human race."

—*The Hartford Courant*

"'Blurbs' demonstrates a fresh talent at play in the fields of his mind. Expert command of the blurb form and a wickedly clever worldview add up to paydirt. Ignore this piece at your own peril!"

—*The San Francisco Chronicle*

"Marked by a rare piquancy, this collection of blurbs sneaks up on you, and before you know it, you're in its clutches. This is fascinating comedy, with energy to spare. Bravo!"

—*The Chicago Tribune*

REELING

Another former student of mine was extremely talented in the musical way. As an undergraduate, he wrote at least a dozen wonderful musicals based on the lives of historical figures. Late last year, I received a package from this young man. Inside was a completed libretto for a musical revue called "Squirrels and Snakes and Other Mistakes," a light-hearted romp in which he lampooned the Lamarckian view of evolution. I was most impressed by the songs, and especially the ballads. If there is a more beautiful song than "My Gray Fluffy Tail," then maybe it is "Every Acorn Is a Bit of Heaven," But these three songs are certainly the three most beautiful songs I have ever heard. I was so impressed by "Squirrels and Snakes and Other Mistakes" that I made my own mistake—I sent a copy of the work along to Mr. Greenman, both to arouse his competitive instincts and to remind him that he should never feel alone when penning humorous musical skits. Two weeks later, he sent me this story, along with a brief note: "Liked funny singing squirrels. Wrote own squirrel piece. Prose." When I confessed my indiscretion to the author of the musical, he fell into a state of deep despair from which he has not yet emerged. I have protested the inclusion of this piece in the collection, not only because it does not rhyme, but because I feel that there is blood on every page.

—*L.O.*

They were a family of squirrels, and they were reeling. There were five, two slightly larger than an average squirrel, two slightly smaller than an average squirrel, and one so small it might have been mistaken for a mouse—except of course by squirrels, who always know their own. The five squirrels sat in the shade of a large oak tree, forest caps and flowers at their feet, and while the smallest squirrel was quite animated—he parted the wet grass with his tiny paws and pushed his nose into the dirt, squealing with delight—the rest of the famliy of squirrels was sad. Sorrowful. Despondent. They were sad because the little one was dead, and the parting of grass and pushing of nose was no more than a dream of what might have been, and not the truth of the matter. How can you speak of a truth of the matter when the matter is squirrels and their sadness? Simple. You look at the crumpled body of the smallest squirrel, you see its eyes gone dull like fogged glass—cold on the inside—you see its fur beginning to drop in tufts from its tail and nape, and you feel the sad pull of truth. Squirrel death is no less real than any other death. With its absence of ceremony, mythology, and sentiment, it is perhaps more real.

A short life is sometimes taken without warning, in a storm, where a cannonade of rain and the noise of blue knives in the sky sends a young squirrel scurrying up an oak, and then the increasing violence of the weather keeps him huddled there, chattering like a baby bird, calling out (to friends? gods?), until the tree itself divides in blinding light. And then the squirrel, scorched in a thin line along his tiny belly, falls to the ground with an odd and understated grace, the wet grass padding the fall, a silence rising off him like smoke from a dying fire. Squirrel, rainstorm, lightning. A trinity that toys with the notion of spirit and then demurs.

The largest of the squirrels, a female, walked in a slow circle around the tiny corpse, careful not to disturb its peace. The peace of the dead is so fragile. Then the other adult squirrel, not quite as fat and not quite as brown, rose up on his back legs. A southern wind blew stiffly, dislodging raindrops from the branches above, releasing them from their captivity so that they fell into the grass around the body. The raindrops vanished inside shallow pools of standing water. The fur of the largest squirrel moved like feathers in the wind. The two smaller squirrels brought nuts and acorns and pebbles, and placed them in patterns around the inert body, patterns that reminded them of games played before the coming of the blue knives in the sky. One nut went underneath the dead squirrel's tiny head, like a pillow whose hardness was itself a form of comfort, proof that even the adamantine world admits a kind of mercy. Of the two squirrels who had collected the nuts and acorns, one retreated from the body, which was beginning to thicken in its joints and face, and retreated to a nearby path, where the two larger squirrels were already assembled. The other did not join the group, choosing instead to stand over the tiny squirrel and brush one paw plantively across its belly, which caught the afternoon sun as it had always caught the afternoon sun, with tiny bursts of light exploding at the tip of every hair. Each hair had a name, produced a sound, made a hopeful promise that it broke as soon as it was swept inside the shade that moved across the body. Whatever the history of a life, it has in its final moments a kind of power—beyond grace, beyond sense—that demands vigilance, and so the squirrel kept watch over his dead brother. The next day, and the day after that, the body would begin to fall away, to leak into the ground, to sanctify the spot where the smallest squirrel had dreamed about pressing his nose into the dirt. For now, the brother, the survivor, the sentinel, waited until darkness had made the color of the body the same as the color of the grass around it, waited until his own gaze matched that of the tiny corpse, waited until the dream dissolved, and then he turned to reclaim his place among his family. But they were gone.

It doesn't seem fair to follow the living squirrel, the small one who stayed behind to tend to a dead brother; there are issues of loyalty, privacy, propriety, and so on. But how can narrative remain fixed upon the dead? Narrative moves—uncertainly sometimes, equivocally always, but inexorably. Time needs another minute, at least. And in that minute, the squirrel, suddenly alone, scurried in the direction he thought his family had gone, toward the city rather than toward the river. He darted through the struts of a bench, skirted an overgrown corner of the park where an aged and feral possum was said to lurk, slipped through ferns, feeling the leaves slicken under his wet nose. In a clearing, he saw another squirrel, and flicked his tail to gain speed, but when he drew nearer he discovered no squirrel at all, only a wet paper bag swaddling a gray wool mitten. A button hung off the mitten like an eye. Where was the other? Lost, probably, unless this was the lost one, and the other was zipped safely within a jacket pocket halfway across town. The squirrel paused and stepped into a blue pool that seemed to have leaked from the moon. Upstart light, a form of trespass, and a way of thieving bravery, until something in the night air broke the moonlight and put a shadow upon his back. What was it? A crooked bough? A bird whose wings remade the night? A memory of loss?

A lost mitten is an accident. A lost child is a tragedy. A lost squirrel is an adventure, charged with possibility, moving like a streamer, faintly risible. He pushed on toward the city, looking for a tree to climb, a bit of food to eat. He had no intention of finding his family any longer. In fact, he had already forgotten them, and remembered only the tiny form of his brother, neck crooked at an angle of alarm, an angle of impossibility, a single thin root running out from beneath his head like a trickle of blood. The memory scraped his heart like rough bark sometimes scraped his belly, and the bird overhead—for it was a bird after all—glanced downward as if the rasp were audible. The squirrel paused, listened to his own quick breaths, put a paw experimentally inside his mouth and made an ugly face. Dark trees flowed upward from the ground until they washed out against the bruise-blue evening sky.

The night became a dance, flowerbeds and streetlights. Dart in front of dog, scurry over newspaper, never wake a sleeping man. The scent of alcohol rose off one man's boots; scarred by scuff marks, they looked like dead things. How was this man different from the tiny squirrel? He was larger—only that. If his brother had been that large, the squirrel would still be waiting for the sun to ignite the final stretch of fur. Would still hope for a divine reprieve. Perhaps it was the tininess that had let him go so easily into death. On a porch, in a garbage can, he found food. Pudding in the porchlight, a half-eaten turkey sandwich squirming in a clear plastic container, bugs lining the yellow edge where the mayonnaise had caked. The squirrel ate hungrily, and when he was full, he curled up in a corner of the porch. A blue light buzzed overhead, more brilliant than the moon, with stripes that made a buzzing noise when bugs entered its mesh. He fell asleep in neon glow, the angry drone of dying flies covered by a sweetness in his ear.

He had a dream. Squirrels dream. A dream of holding, and of being held, of curling up alongside a body much like his own, but somehow different. He understood that this was his tiny brother grown. His dream was mostly eyes, his tiny brother's eyes, and the way they shaped to wonder and to joy. He had lagged behind then the other four took brisk walks. He had collected extra acorns, unnecessary food, against the laws of nature. He had been born too close to death. Then he was tiny again. He held a walnut in his mouth, and then swallowed it whole. His body shook, his throat stretched as if it would burst, but the acorn went down and stayed down. The dreaming squirrel could see the contours of the nut inside his brother's belly; the fur along its curve was charred and bristled. When the acorn was down, the tiny squirrel clapped both paws over his mouth, then thrust them violently away in a gesture of announcement. From his open mouth a stream of flies emerged, propelled by fetid breath. One of the flies was a bird.

When the squirrel woke, it was early morning, and the clank of pots inside the house sent him scampering off the porch. At a nearby pond, he washed his paws, and then walked across a narrow strip of beach to dry them. The beach had black sand so fine he could not hear his own footfalls in the silt. A pane of glass, nicked at two of his corners, leaned against a tree stump, and he stood on his legs and looked inside it. He knew this was his own reflection, the almond-shaped eyes, the tight brown patch of fur upon the brow, but when he touched a paw to the pane he wasn't sure. He bared his teeth in mock anger, part of a game he used to play with his brother. How do you take a game for two and learn to play with one? You start, and you never stop. The squirrel kept his paw upon the pane, saw a mouse run through the dry grass next to the lake, pushed his paw harder into the reflection. He knew it was his own. If he saw other squirrels, he would account them as large mice. He was lost inside the glass. His own family would mean nothing to him. He was with his brother in his loneliness. He would never understand. He could not miss him any more, or any less.

HART HURTS HIS HAND

Hart's ex-wife is at the Villa Centobrenci with a new lover who is the scion of an Italian copper dynasty; his last girl-friend is sending him letters that say things like "I have that reddish brownish shirt of yours and don't know what to do with it" and "You know that bird you bought for me? It died"; and Hart himself is shifting uncomfortably in an army-issue chair in Alexandria, Virginia, slaving away on a memo about the recent advances in the delivery of Permanent Change of Station packets. Say a soldier is sent from Fort Bragg to Fort Gillem. Say that same soldier, three months later, receives orders to report for duty at Fort Kastamasta at oh six hundred hours Monday morning. Even a year earlier, that soldier would have depended upon the U.S. Mail to deliver a thick packet that not only contained classified information about the strategic justification for the reassignment, but also described the soldier's new sur-roundings, the restaurants, the bars, the video rental estab-lishments. Without that packet, the soldier would be lost. Where could he get his car washed with the assurance that it would be properly waxed? Would he be able to find his way to the local church on Sunday morning? Once, Hart had been one of those men on the Bragg-Gillem-Kastamasta treadmill. He had been adrift in the sea of confusion the army called "standard transfer," or "ship-out," or "PCS," which stands for "Permanent Change of Station." Permanent: Ha. Is permanent nine blissful months in Georgia rudely shattered by a corpulent sergeant who barks a peremptory Texas directive that sours the scent of the peach pie that lingers, still fragrant, in your nose? Is permanent a weekend of headache and stomachache, a weekend without the appearance in your mailbox of a single manila envelope from Army brass, let alone the all-important PCS packet?

Hart has a ball he bounces off the wall behind his desk. Sometimes it bounces off the desk and then caroms off the wall: Ka-thop! Sometimes it bounces off the wall and back into his hand: Thop! Sometimes it equivocates fatally, missing both the plane of the desk and the plane of the wall, instead making for the corner and, shivering there for a moment, popping back out without confidence, stumbling over a stapler or a pen and then skittering left or right, undignified, dystrophic: Fritz!

Hart's right arm has a strip of red on its underside just behind the bone of his wrist. At first, Hart thought it was a rash, and thought about going to the infirmary, but he eventually figured out that it was a line that marked the place where the edge of the desk cut into the skin. He felt foolish, but he reminded himself that a rash was indeed one of the possible diagnoses. He had suffered from rashes before, once when he was a child, and his mother kept him home from school, and once when he went away to school. At the time, he was a quiet young man who did not yet have any notion of what adulthood might bring him. His roommate, a curly haired, brawny Oklahoman named Alan Leacock who liked to say that he was going to "beer college," was the first to notice the rash. "Damn," he said. "There's something nasty on your arm. You're going to die, man." Hart went to the doctor, who was an attractive young woman, and when she told him to take off his shirt so she could see the extent of the rash, he turned his back to her in shame so that she would not see his sunken chest. In the clinic, Hart resolved, as he had a hundred times before, to eat more and exercise more so that he would fill out. But the medicine the doctor prescribed upset his stomach, and he could not eat even as much as he had before, and he was too tired to exercise.

Hart heard later that Alan had gone to see the doctor for an injury sustained while lifting weights, and that he had asked her out. "You should have seen how she was looking at me," Alan said. "She knew I had the goods." Then Alan went off singing a country song he had composed called, "I Had the Goods and She Wanted Me Bad." Like everything he had ever sung, it was awful. Later on, Alan reinjured himself during a football scrimmage and decided to devote himself to his music. "If I don't make it as a musician," he said, "I can always work in a car lot." He worked in a car lot just outside of St. Louis. "It's great here," he liked to say when Hart called him. "I'm a manager now. Soon it'll be Alan Leacock Motors."

Hart's last girlfriend was named Ellen Leacock. "What a coincidence," he said when he met her. "I know," she said, which threw him a bit until he realized she was joking. That was always the case with Ellen—jokes that didn't quite hang together, like the thing about the bird, which confused Hart, because he didn't remember buying her one. Ellen liked to joke, she said, because it was the only thing that prevented her from throwing herself into a gulch. "A deep, deep, deep, deep gulch," she said. "Get what I mean? It's deep." One of the first times they went out, he took her to a crab shack, and as soon as they were seated, she began to pelt him with inquiries: where his parents were born, what he liked most about his childhood, whether or not he was adventurous about foods when he traveled. He told her that she asked too many questions. "What the hell gives you that idea?" she said. "Huh? I mean, was it something I said?" Hart wanted to take her dancing, but he didn't know of any local dance clubs. "Where can we go?" he asked, waving his arms. "You know that you're shouting, right?" she said. "No," he said, telling the truth. "Well, you are," she said. "Anyway, we can still go somewhere. We can go to my house." They went. A sprinkler in the backyard sent a light spray against her bedroom window, where Hart stood and watched Ellen undress for the first time. Once he would have been as shy on her behalf as he was on his own, but he had learned to summon up courage at moments like these. "Stop looking at me!" Ellen shrieked, and Hart nearly fainted. "Kidding," she said. "Just kidding. I'm ninety-nine percent kidding."

Hart liked Ellen because, like Hart, she liked numbers that were one less than the numbers that other people liked. Other people like one hundred; Hart likes ninety-nine.

Other people like five and ten and twenty; Hart is all about four and nine and nineteen. He wonders if this means that he is a lesser man, or if it means he is a greater man, because he does not need the comfort of large numbers. Hart once knew a man who was hot for one-hundred-and-one, or one-thousand-and-one, or eleven. He was a captain whose wife was widely known to be the kind of woman who would pop right up in another man's bed, her unhooked brassiere dangling from one smooth shoulder. He had called up Alan, who was his only friend from college, and told him about the captain. "That poor bastard," Alan said. He had gotten married a few years after college, to a short, broad-shouldered woman named Meg who seemed to siphon off everything that was loud and obnoxious—everything that was Alan-about Alan. "Can you imagine the way he feels? He's got a wife he probably loves, and she spends her time with other men. It's awful." Hart had a sudden thought that Alan might not be talking about the captain at all. He invented an excuse and hung up the telephone. There was something about Alan's tone that made him want to turn away, the way he had turned away from people who were undressing.

Hart's chair, while uncomfortable, is not the worst chair he has ever had. The worst was while he was stationed in Alabama, working on a policy that renamed EFMP clinics as EDIS facilities and limited enrollment in EDIS-C programs to IDEA-eligible patients. In Alabama, Hart's back hurt like a son of a bitch after the long days of typing. He had headaches that he was certain were related to his backaches, and hand cramps that just wouldn't let up. He didn't even have a ball to bounce, because the ranking officer was a man who claimed to have special sensitivity to annoying noises and would not tolerate so much as a transistor radio. Hart heard he came to harm in Atlanta soon after explaining the new EDIS policy to a bunch of upper brass. Something about a car wreck. Three days later, the ranking officer's replacement came to the office. "Hello," she said. Hart forced his eyes up from the policy memo, and saw a woman who was thirty-five at most, slim, attractive, and possessed of a tiny bow of a mouth that, more than anything, drew him in. Then she married him. Or so he liked to tell Alan, when the truth was that it was a slightly longer process: She looked him up and down, she asked him to her office to discuss the protocol of the policy department, she suggested that they continue the conversation over dinner, she unclipped her hair in a way that was, if stagy, also undeniably effective, and then she married him. Her name was Carrie, and the moment that Hart first understood the extent of her interest in him was the same moment that it first occurred to Hart that he might be attractive to women. "Yeah, right," said Alan, who was separated from Meg and back to his old self. "What? Is she blind? You're a goddamned scarecrow. Maybe she's a vulture looking for a quick meal."

Hart cannot think about Carrie. He has made a solemn pledge, a vow to himself, to avoid the topic. But his mind, while it respects the letter of his laws, does not respect their spirit, and it drifts into a memory of the Villa Centobrenci, the Italian inn where Hart unwittingly introduced his wife to Giovanni Megna, the dashing young bachelor with the sparkle in his eyes and the ability, it was said, "to make sweet poetry of copper piping." They had been travelling on a delayed honeymoon, and Megna had been a gracious host. He had spoken with great admiration of the American army and its role in promoting European industry. "Italy is thought of for its copper coins, its copper pots, its copper-engraved maps," Megna had said. "But did you know that this versatile metal has also been responsible for saving the lives of tens of thousands of American soldiers, not to mention two Presidents?" He did not elaborate. Instead, he invited Hart's wife upstairs to see his collection of seventeenth-century majolica pitchers. Hart sat downstairs and read a magazine. He stretched his legs out underneath a copper table and sipped water from a copper cup. He lifted a copper plate that was engraved around the edge with an Italian slogan that meant nothing to him, and used it as a mirror. He was happy to be out of Germany, happy to be in Italy. He thought he might eat a pizza, or a proscuitto-and-fontina panini. He had no jealousy in him. Now, years later, he curses that magazine-reading, leg-stretching, copper-cup-holding, pizza-and-panini-desiring numbskull. He bounces the ball off the wall: Thop! Thop! Thop!

Hart's marriage ended like a movie ended. "I can't do this," Carrie said over dinner a week after she went upstairs to see Giovanni Megna's majolica pitchers. They were still at the Villa Centobrenci. Then she lowered her head to her hands and wept. Hart stared at her, certain the scene would fade to black, or that he would hear the tick of film against the projector bar that signalled that it was time for a new reel. Hart thought about overturning the table, but realized that it was too heavy; he had no interest in straining to lift a corner of the table while his wife put her head down on another corner and shut her eyes to their recently deceased marriage. "I think that certain situations aren't meant to be," said Alan, who had reconciled with Meg. "I think that everyone has a heart that is a certain shape, and it either fits with the heart of another person or it doesn't." "That's stupid," said Hart, hoping to goad Alan into some good-natured cruelty. "Maybe," Alan said morosely, and Hart hung up.

Hart came back to America, and to his desk in Alabama, which had seemed ugly and small before but now seemed even uglier and smaller, like a tiny garbage barge. The office was no better: It was filled with filing cabinets that were filled with drawers. Only a fraction of them had ever been opened. Then he was transferred to Georgia, and to Ellen, where he had an office he did not even remember, because it was not the point of Georgia. Then he came to Alexandria, where his office quickly came to feel like a twin of the Alabama office. "You can come and visit, you know," he said to Ellen on the telephone. "No phone calls," she said, like she was a spy. "Very dangerous. Must only write letters." This time, Hart was sure she was joking, but when he called her back later, she said, "Can't stress point strongly enough. Letters only." Hart sputtered something: "Wait," or "But," or "Well." "Will not repeat self again," Ellen said. "Also, write them in longhand. It makes me feel better."

Hart's hand sometimes cramps toward the end of a letter. He works in this small office all by himself from eight in the morning to seven in the evening, breaking for an hour for a lunch that usually consists of a sandwich from the cafeteria and a cup of near-boiling coffee. Hart used to relax in the afternoons, to put his feet up on his desk, read the paper, maybe call Alan. But now Alan is a father, and his resignation is even more profound than when he was only a husband, and the times when he will attack Hart are even rarer, and Hart isn't sure what the point of calling him would be. Plus, this PCS project, which Hart initially assumed was a bureaucratic lark, the kind of thing a C.O. assigns to an officer to plump up budgets, had been upgraded to a UDI, an Urgent Document Initiative. As a result, the only way that Hart can break the monotony is to write letters to Ellen, which he does. Usually, he only gets through about a paragraph a day. A full letter takes about a week. She never responds with a letter of her own, although once a month or so she will call him and leave him an encouraging message on his answering machine, usually in the same clipped spy-speak: "Still have feelings," or "Degree of affection detected," or "Must know that I am undressing now."

Hart knows that no one can see him in his office. He sometimes fantasizes about hidden security cameras that monitor his every move, but he quickly realizes that this is a dream of self-aggrandizement, in which his moves are important enough to be monitored. Whatever quality-of-life improvements result from his work, Hart does not, deep down, believe that they warrant round-the-clock surveillance. When he makes peace with this idea, and remembers that no one is watching him, he likes to dance. In the afternoon, when his coffee is cold, he gets up out of his chair, just pushes that wretched hunk of plush and plastic to one side, and puts his hands up by his shoulders. Then he slides his right foot to the right side, slides his left foot in beside his right, slides to the right a second time, shakes his hips, shimmies his shoulders, then slides the right foot back to meet the left and steps in place twice. All the while he hums to himself, songs that remind him of the ballads Alan made up in college. They have lyrics, although Hart doesn't like to sing them out loud. One is called "Italy Has Brittled Me and Virginia Is No Better." One is called "The BS of PCS." One is called "I Had a Ball and Then I Bounced It Off the Wall." Hart's wife hadn't liked the same kind of music as Hart. She liked big-band music, orchestras with tootling horns and thundering drums. Hart couldn't abide it, still can't. He wonders if Giovanni Megna is a swing man.

Hart's day, especially after dancing, can stretch until it seems like an eternity. Hart wishes that he could work up the desire to call Alan. He wants someone to come and get him, to drive to Alexandria in a new car from his dealership, to turn onto the base, pull up outside Hart's office, and honk the horn. "Coming," Hart will say, and then he'll go. If there are papers on his desk that need filing, forms that need filling out, well, then the next guy will just have to do it. Hart also wishes that he could work up the courage to call Ellen. Instead, he tacks another paragraph onto the current letter and then folds it and slips it into the top drawer of his garbage-barge desk.

Hart kicks his chair. He doesn't know what else to do. He has requested a new chair a thousand times, not only in Alexandria but in other places, in Alabama, in Georgia, and his requests have never been answered, let alone denied. During his separation from Meg, Alan had an idea about the chair. "Steal one from someone else," he said. "Just walk right in and take it. People won't know what to do about it. They're not equipped to handle chair-stealing." Hart explained that they were equipped, that they would just discipline him, dock his pay, threaten him with various kinds of punishment. "Fine, then," Alan said. "Just sit in the goddamned chair until your organs rot and leak out of your body." Hart spins around in his chair, fairly certain that he has almost reached this point.

Hart's ideas about himself haven't changed since he was seventeen. Back then, he thought that he was too skinny, with a certain sunken look around the eyes that gave him the appearance of being thoughtful and a tendency to get overexcited when he talked. "A scarecrow," Alan had said. "You know you're shouting, right?" Ellen had said. When Hart looks in the mirror now, he sees the same man. But there is no mirror in sight—no mirror mounted over the desk, no mirror on the back wall, no mirror tucked behind the coatrack. Though he has not opened every drawer, Hart is ninety-nine percent sure there is no mirror anywhere in the room. So who is the man who sits down after dancing, thinks of his ex-wife and his last girlfriend, mourns the fact that one ever entered his life and that the other may have exited it, tries to imagine them both naked but fails entirely in one case and partially in the other, considers dancing again but decides against it out of pure inertia, takes a sip of cold coffee despite the fact that he knows it will displease him, bounces the ball off the desk and the wall (ka-thop!), watches as the ball spins right, lunges for it, bangs his hand against the edge of his computer monitor, releases a fusillade of invective, massages his injured knuckle, takes another sip of coffee, and finally capitulates to the PCS-packet-delivery memo on his desk, the memo that outlines a new policy that some believe will revolutionize the way that soldiers are notified of their transfers and acclimated into their new communities?

FRAGMENTS FROM *ELECTION!*
THE MUSICAL

Though it was predicted with uncanny precision by Professor Onge, the explosion of interest in the fake musical form that followed the publication of my Elian Gonzalez musical would be difficult for me to believe if I did not witness it firsthand. It made the first wave of interest in my musicals look like a tiny, tiny chair next to a much, much larger chair. Some extremely famous people called me personally and begged me to write fake celebrity musicals as star vehicles for them. "No, Gwyneth," I said, or "No, Mr. Hope. I will not write another musical. This I swear." But then the United States held a Presidential election that devolved into absurdity and left the nation without a leader. Mr. Hope, who was still on the phone line—I think he probably forgot to hang up— said "Hey, this would be funny." He was right, I suppose, although I hate him for it.

With no great enthusiasm, I wrote a piece about the election and buried it in my desk drawer, unhappy that I had capitulated but happy that I could at least conceal my capitulation. As luck would have it, though, Professor Onge was visiting my home, helping me to collect the material for this book. He found this musical and, without my permission, mailed it to the publisher.

—B.G.

FRAGMENTS FROM ELECTION! THE MUSICAL

{The curtain rises on a news reporter standing before the national electoral map.}

NEWS REPORTER:
Over my two decades in the business
Some of my work has been just superb.
I once did a piece
On the civil war in Greece
And then there was the series on the Serbs.

This year, I thought that I'd take it easy,
Sit behind a desk election night.
Watch the exit polls
Eat a bunch of coffee rolls.
The race, they said, would probably be tight.

{The night before the election, the candidates appear before their campaigns.}

GORE:
I plan to win.
The country knows
What shape it's in.

BUSH:
I will prevail.
If that means "win,"
I cannot fail.

{The night of the election, the news media awaits the results.}

NEWS REPORTER:
Florida goes for Gore.
Bush's hopes are slim.
In the Electoral score
Things are looking grim.

Florida's swinging back.
Our earlier pronouncement
Has come under attack.
Please wait for an announcement.

Bush has Florida now.
He will win the race.
We cannot say just how.
This egg got on our face.

Scratch that "Bush Wins" news.
Scratch this whole election.
This vaunted right to choose
Is democracy's infection.

{The day after the election, voters across the country are confused, but nowhere more than in Florida.}

FLORIDA VOTER:
I'd rather be shot from a cannon
Than vote for that Nazi Buchanan.
I thought that I voted for Gore

But I just don't know anymore.

{Days pass without decisive results.}

NEWS REPORTER:
An election with no President
Is like a perfume with no scent
Or a spice rack with no salt or pepper.

BILL CLINTON:
Hey, jackass! Don't get too upset
I'm not done as Big Chief yet.
I'm a lame duck, buddy, not a leper!

{KATHERINE HARRIS, Florida Secretary of State, vows to get to the bottom of the election results. The media descends upon Florida to watch as recounts begin.}

KATHERINE HARRIS:
Nice to meet you.
Nice to meet you.
Yes, I have okayed
Some limited recounting.

Nice to meet you.
Nice to meet you.
Yes, the pressure on me
Is steadily mounting.

THE MEDIA:
Day one was fun.
Day two was, too.
Day three and day four were exciting for Gore.
Day five and day six smacked of dirty tricks.
Days seven and eight, we awaited our fate.
Day nine and day ten, we started over again.

KATHERINE HARRIS:
Nice to meet you.
Nice to meet you.
In the state GOP
My star is ascendant.

Nice to meet you.
Nice to meet you.
Do you think that I look
Like a flight attendant?

THE MEDIA:
Day thirteen, day thirteen
Cigarettes and caffeine
Are the only things keeping us awake.
Day fourteen, day fourteen
That damned voting machine!
We've had about all we can take.

KATHERINE HARRIS:
Nice to meet you.
Nice to meet you.

I thank you all so much
For enduring this frustration.

Nice to meet you.
Nice to meet you.
I will soon have results
To bring before the nation.

*{KATHERINE HARRIS calls a meeting to announce
Florida's final tallies.}*

KATHERINE HARRIS:
I said that I'd be calm.
I said that I'd be cool.
I said that I'd be smooth
I wouldn't act the fool.

Well, I lied.
Because he's certified.
I swear to you he's certified.
This feeling that I have inside
Can't be denied
I feel like a beautiful new bride!
George W. Bush is
Cer-ti-fied!!!

{The candidates react to the announcement.}

BUSH:
Some people pay attention in the classroom

Others like to have a real good time.
(What's the point of being rich and famous
If partying is treated as a crime?)
At any rate, I wasn't much for schoolbooks.
But there's one thing that is clear as a bell:
Parents pass along traits like height and brains.
My daddy gave me something else as well:
I am President.
I am President.
Because of that, the other guy is not.
I am President.
I am President.
I got more in the college than he got.

They say that I'm stupid and dullish and dense
But I understand things that make perfect sense.

I am President.
I am President.
Because of that the other guy is not.
I am President.
I am President.
I got more in the college than he got.

Number One.
It's so fun.
Like father, like son!

GORE:
In these kinds of environments

It's very customary

To speak in rhyming prose or even sing.

But I fear that such a practice

Will simply blur the issue

Which is that the results mentioned by Ms. Harris include illegal votes

And do not include legal votes that were improperly rejected.

The number of such votes is more than sufficient to place in doubt

The result of this election.

Thank you.

A BIG FIGHT SCENE BETWEEN TWO MEN WITH THE SAME NAME

Ray hit Ray on the shoulder first, and then Ray hit Ray on the nose. This sent Ray reeling, but as he fell backward he managed to rake his right arm across Ray's face, opening up a cut to the immediate left of Ray's nose. Ray still had the upper hand, though, and shoved Ray hard with both hands, finalizing Ray's fall to the ground. For a few seconds, Ray stood over Ray in triumph. When Ray bent down to exult over Ray's fallen body, though, Ray grabbed his hair, which Ray wore long, and tugged it as hard as he could. Ray collapsed next to Ray on the floor, and Ray jumped up quickly and began kicking Ray. Ray wore boots, and he used the hard point and the heel expertly, not kicking Ray in the ribs but rather working the tender areas around the kidneys. Ray found a metal ruler on the ground, and managed to whack Ray across the shins, and then to bury the corner of the ruler in Ray's knees. At that, Ray collapsed in pain, and, clutching his knee, lost his balance. His downward progress had serious consequences for Ray; Ray's knees were propelled into Ray's throat, and Ray groaned and rolled over onto his side. Ray crawled toward the door, convinced that the blunt force of his knees upon Ray's neck had finished Ray off, but as he stretched his hand toward the knob, he felt an explosion at the base of his neck. It was Ray. He was brandishing a pool cue—where on earth had that come from, Ray wondered? Ray struck Ray with the cue twice against the back of the head, and then held it like a battering ram, with the tapered end toward Ray. Ray drew himself to his feet and rushed at Ray with all his strength. The maneuver had the desired effect, driving the tip of the cue back into Ray—in fact, into his left hip, where it ripped Ray's shirt and tore into Ray's skin. Ray stood; though his legs were wobbly, he felt his strength returning. He faced off against Ray, who had also pulled himself to his feet, and the two of them began raining blows on one another. Ray's fist went into Ray's eye. Ray's fist went into Ray's ear. Ray gouged at Ray's eyes. Ray got Ray in a headlock and thumped his nose with the flat of his palm. Ray's hands were slick with Ray's blood, and Ray wondered how much longer Ray could go on like this.

STRUGGLE IN NINE

I.

Cautious, he picked up the magazine. Interested, he read it from cover to cover. Amused, he laughed. Transfixed, he gasped. Gratified, he wrote a letter to the editor commending the magazine. Eager, he picked up the next month's issue. Surprised, he found that his letter was printed in the Letters to the Editor column. Emboldened, he wrote another one. Amazed, he saw that his second letter was printed as well. He took a long look in the mirror. The mirror had a flaw on the righthand side that always looked like a scar on his skin. He traced the scar with his right hand. Altered, he was. Altered, and changed. What he had been before, he no longer remained.

II.

The eagle of communism swooped down and grabbed the rabbit of capitalism. The general woke up sweating. He grabbed his gun and ran into the garden. Was there an Arab? Was there a killer? Was there a point to be made? The general sat down on a bench and hung his head. In movies he had seen, generals were always brave. They were often corrupt, but they were always brave. Their faces turned red when they were accused of cowardice. They pounded their fists on tables and stood ramrod-straight when they inspected the troops. The general felt an ant skirt the flannel edge of his pajamas and he began to shriek, for ants had killed his son and now they were coming for him.

III.

Girl in bar: Are you a good writer?
Me: Yeah. I mean, I think so. I have good ideas and attach good words to them.
Girl in bar: I am a good dancer.
Me: Really?
Girl in bar: No. Not really. But when girls say they are dancers, boys tend to like it.
Me: That's funny. That's why I said I was a writer.
Girl in bar: You're not?
Me: No, I am. But that's why I said it. Sometimes there are happy coincidences.

IV.

I have a friend. She writes miniatures. I love them. I love her. Her pieces are short. Ten words at most. But they sing. This piece, the piece I am writing, is already too long. Even

Section IV is too long. "You are bloated and incontinent," she said. "You don't know how to control yourself. A story is about a flower that bends slightly under the breath of a dog. No more than that. 'A flower bends slightly under the breath of a dog.' Man, that's long. I want to cut out some words. I will cut out 'slightly.' Now it has nine words. Now I am happier with it. Will you take me to dinner to celebrate?" We go to dinner. We drink too much wine. We end up at her place, on her couch. She takes my head in her hands. My lips rise to meet hers.

V.

Birds don't write. They are God's creatures, of course, and God's chosen creatures, in some sense, for they fly more closely to His Divine Providence than any of us can hope to, but despite their privileged station they cannot write. When they see a rabbit on the ground, they can only choose whether or not to kill it. Is this a form of writing? It is certainly a plot. It most certainly reveals character. Time, someone once told me, is what keeps everything from happening all at once. History, I retorted, is what ensures that everything has happened. We each thought ourselves the cleverer.

VI.

I have a friend. She writes miniatures. She tells me that my pieces have too much plot. I cannot understand what she means. To my eye, they have no plot. "You are always sending and receiving like a radio station or a radio," she says. "You are always doing what should never be done. I am going to put on my pants and leave." She leaves. I turn on the radio. There is a song on the radio about a girl who leaves. I turn off the radio. There is a bird flying outside. It banks in the air and heads right toward my window. I close my eyes, afraid of what I will see.

VII.

Me: Yes, I do love you. But not the way you need me to. I think that sometimes you're too afraid.

Girl in bar: I was afraid of that.

Me: Not everything is a joke. That's why I wish you wouldn't talk.

Girl in bar: Yes. I know. But when a girl decides not to talk, she disappears. And I'm afraid of disappearing.

Me: Really?

Girl in bar: That's why I never finish anything I start, so that there's a reason still to be here.

Me: No. I mean, I don't understand. You leave things undone so that you will not vanish? You're in a bad way.

Girl in bar: Are you in a good way?

VIII.

The third of March fell on the second of March. It wasn't a very common occurrence, and as such it was noteworthy. The man on the telephone was eager to make a sale, and so he divulged the secrets of the calendar. Would the lady be interested in learning how one day became the next? Did she possess an understanding of midnight? The man on the telephone hung up and took a deep breath. Most of the women he called demonstrated no interest in the calendar. They asked him if he knew of a place they could buy shoes, or books. Occasionally they had a thing for carpets. The man felt the telephone looking at him and felt afraid. He pounded a fist on the table and felt even more afraid. He picked up a magazine and began to read.

IX.

When he began to read, he knew that he would soon begin to write. But when he began to write, he knew he would not finish. Would not, and could not. He forced his mind ahead in time. He saw the seam where the day turned into the next day, and tried to imagine that his writing was a bridge across that seam, which was widening by the second. He saw the scar where one day was ripped away from the day that had preceded it. He went for a walk. He sat down, exhausted. He continued on again, rested. He searched for a place to stop and eat, famished. He spoke to an old man in uniform, lonely. He spoke to a pretty girl, attracted. He wandered, disoriented. He saw a bird, comforted. He thought it God, converted.

IN SHUVALOV'S LIBRARY

I have written earlier of my doubts about Mr. Greenman's suitability for historical fiction. Here is the crowning example: a story about the eminent eighteenth-century scholar Ivan Ivanovich Shuvalov, the founder of Moscow University and the architect of the Empress Elizaveta Petrovna's library, the vast artistic and literary holdings of which were once the pride of Europe. Shuvalov has always struck me as a fascinating subject for a piece of literature, and I have, for years, urged my students and colleagues to build a work around him, ideally a comic work with plenty of singing. When Mr. Greenman announced that he was writing a short story about Shuvalov, I was simultaneously filled with surprise and trepidation: surprise because I did not see how a nonmusical treatment could do justice to Shuvalov, and trepidation because I feared that a nonmusical work would foreclose all musical possibilities. Still, I sent Mr Greenman extensive notes about Shuvalov, both as a scholar and as a man—notes that were, evidently, discarded, because the work that finally emerged from his labors was this rather airy farrago, which has not a single song. If you, the reader, can listen to this work, then perhaps you can also be honest with yourself: Would it have been helped or harmed by a series of clever couplets? Perhaps the first could have been "Ivan the Red / Was filled with dread."

—*L.O.*

He knew English. That's why it was troubling, the "I" that he inked inside the front cover of every volume, before every occurrence of his last name. But it was not troubling on its own. It was troubling for the dollop of punctuation that followed, designed as a period but slyly canted in the direction of a comma. "I, Shuvalov," he wrote, and set down his pen.

A line of seventy words joined him to the Empress. "Elizaveta Petrovna," he wrote, and then wrote sixty-eight words more. Among them were the words "acquisition," "collection," and "artistry." The line of words was also a line of argument: He was reminding the empress that he needed a building in which he could display the paintings, sculptures, and rare books he had collected over the years. "I have noted many times that acquisition itself is a form of artistry," he said, "and for that alone I should need a museum."

In the years since he had come to court—more than ten years, he said whenever he was asked—Shuvalov made the same request every week; that was how things were done with the Empress. He already had the record of the museum: His catalog was comprehensive, and included every book, painting, etching, sculpture, and *object d'art* that he had persuaded the Empress to purchase. "Collection" was the title he had given to the first book, and "Collection, Section II" to its successor. He had filled four volumes thus far, all leather-bound, and was now working on the fifth section. Just that morning he had entered a painting that showed a solitary man alone in a room, gazing out a high, small window. The room was drab and poorly lit; the world outside the window was dominated by a round, green tree, the branches of which sparkled with brightly colored birds.

Shuvalov knew why he was attracted to the painting. He even looked a bit like the man in the room; he had the same deep-set eyes, the same strong chin. The man in the room was handsome, as was Shuvalov himself. But he felt as if the painting misrepresented the truth. In his mind, the world inside his study was far superior, because it contained hundreds of possibilities, whereas the world outside the window was limited to a single existence, fixed by the artist's imagination. The painting was attributed to an artist named Bassano, a lesser contemporary of Tintoretto, though one of the previous owners had endeavored to prove that it was the work of the master himself. Shuvalov was not in the business of judging these kinds of claims; he had merely noted it in the margins of his entry and moved on. Even if he had been able to determine whether or not the painting was a Tintoretto, he could not have done so from his study: Like most of the works in the Collection, it was elsewhere in the palace. He had only notes that described it: scraps of paper, letters submitted by other members of the court, his own jottings. Taken as a set, they added up to the painting; the sum of all these words was a picture.

The method by which the Collection was created was painstaking. Another man might have devised a quicker procedure, but for Shuvalov the success of a process came from the amount of control it demanded of its operator. From the various documents of description, he transferred the name of each work, its medium, a brief characterization, the date it came into the possession of the Empress, its previous provenance, and so forth. He assigned each work a number, and determined whether any other works were related, either by artist, by period, or by subject. "This Collection," he had written to the Empress in one of his earlier letters, "will one day itself be recognized as an artwork—then, perhaps, it, too, can be entered into the Collection." One small stroke of cleverness was enough for Shuvalov. He concluded the letter and sealed it.

.   .   .

When Shuvalov had first arrived at court, he had not permitted visitors into his chambers. "It is a sanctuary," he had announced to the attentive circle of eyes and ears. His youth had attracted visitors, and not just his youth, but the way it conspired with his high position in the court to produce a collar of importance around him. "It is a sanctuary, and that is why it must be located at the end of the longest hall in the palace." He tried to affect a lonely air.

The ladies of the court had taken an immediate interest in him, both as a result of his solitary nature and as a result of his appearance; he was told by the women, even the Empress herself, that he was a handsome man. One woman had a profile that was a lesson in severity but was unaccountably beautiful. Another woman had wide eyes that were always in a state of agitation. Shuvalov remembered asking her to close her eyes and then he remembered kissing the lids softly. Beneath his lips, the lids had the feel of butterflies. A third woman had a strong back upon which his fingers moved slowly, as if half-asleep. When he took his leave after an assignation, Shuvalov would go directly to his chambers; he would use the walk down the hall to recover every detail of the woman, naming his memories, filing them.

But all this was long ago, when he had first come to court. Over the years, Shuvalov had observed that the women at court seemed to desire his company less and less. He still came to court, because his presence was required, but he no longer needed to affect a lonely air. His loneliness was actual, and some days palpable.

Though Shuvalov's life at court was without women, the circle around him had not dissipated. Where women once stood, there were now men, and they touched their beards thoughtfully as Shuvalov spoke, and murmured noises of agreement or dissent. The faces of the men had changed regularly for a number of years, and then, for a number of years, they had stayed the same. There was Prince Pyotor, who had lost a foot in combat and descanted bitterly on a wide range of topics; Prince Alexsandr, a small man who smoked small cigars that he gripped between his stained teeth; and Prince Sergei, a thin man who liked to let loose a high, pealing laugh that was as wild as his hair, which hung around his head like the mane of a lion. The three of them had asked him more about the library, over a longer period of time, than anyone else, and this familiarity had encouraged a sort of presumption. The princes had, as long as Shuvalov could remember, asked him when he might allow them to see this majestic book, the Collection, that contained within it a full account of all the artwork that had earned the approval of the crown. "Never," Shuvalov said. He had explained his reasoning so many times that he no longer felt it necessary to elaborate.

• • •

When Shuvalov was not making entries in the ledgers of the Collection, he liked to read in philosophy, usually Augustine, which filled him with a mixture of sorrow and satisfaction. Like Augustine, he believed in setting aside parts of the self to strengthen the remaining parts. That was why the Bassano bothered him; it suggested that when the man was done mastering the contents of the room, he could simply go to the window and be delivered into a new world. Shuvalov believed otherwise. A man could cast his lot either with the room or with the window, but not both. He caressed the skin of Collection, Section V and turned his chair so that he faced the door to his study.

Shuvalov stared at the door. For years, he had thought nothing of it; it was merely a mahogany panel interposed between him and the long hall, the longest in the palace, the hall where he made peace daily with his solitude. Recently, though, as he came down the long hall, he began to feel as though he was being followed. At first, it was just a vague suspicion, but then, one day, he had heard the sound of footfalls behind him, moving at the same rate that he moved. When he turned around, though, he saw no one, and it did not seem to matter how fast he turned around— he could not catch so much as a glimpse of a figure darting into one of the small side rooms that lined the hall. When he resumed walking, the sound behind him also resumed, and it took a great deal of concentration, applied over a number of days, before he could be certain that it was not simply the sound of his own footsteps, trailing behind him by some accident of acoustics. That same analysis seemed to rule out certain suspects: It was unlikely to be Pyotor, for his peg would not only have given his gait a different sound but would have prevented him from moving quickly; similarly, Shuvalov was fairly certain that he would have noticed Sergei's wild hair, or that something about the situation would have induced the prince to let go with one of his wild blasts of laughter.

His inability to solve the mystery of the footsteps did not bother him, for the footsteps were not the problem. Or rather, they were not the extent of the problem. For they were only the cocking of the trigger; the firing of the weapon was the knocking that came on the door of his chambers every afternoon, a sharp report that sounded so loudly that he thought it might be his own bones banging together. The first time it had happened, he had flinched violently and accidentally dragged his pen across a catalog entry for a Bruyn landscape, disfiguring it. Works had been dispatched from the Empress's holdings before through sale, or extracted through theft, and their catalog records had been deleted accordingly, but this was the first time that Shuvalov could remember nullifying one of the entries in the Collection as a result of his own error. He sat at his desk, his heart pounding, waiting for a second knock, but none came.

Until, that is, the next day, which brought another single knock, another blow to his heart: He had stood quickly and pulled the door open, but no one was there. The third day, too, he had opened the door after the knock to find an empty hallway. Then he began to notice that the knock was coming at the same time each day, at exactly two o'clock. The fifth day, he set aside the Collection at ten minutes to two and crouched by the door, ready to fling it open. The knock came at two; he opened the door; he found nothing. And each morning, as he came down the long hall to his chambers, the footsteps were still there, evasive, impossible to certify, like a face in a dream.

Though the footsteps irritated him and the knocking terrified him, Shuvalov discussed neither phenomenon at court. If the culprit was present there, his disclosure would only be a source of malicious pleasure. Whether or not the knocking was a subject of conversation, it was quickly becoming apparent to Shuvalov that it was disrupting his daily routine. He found that he could not concentrate in the late morning and early afternoon, because his anticipation was so powerful. Some days he tried to brace himself for the noise. Other days he tried to ignore it. Nothing he did seemed to have any effect. Soon, Shuvalov began to lose sleep at night, and that took an even greater toll during the day—he was in a stage of nervous agitation while he was walking through the palace taking down the particulars of paintings or sculptures that had been acquired but not yet fully recorded. Worse, he began to make errors in his entries: spelling errors, errors in date of acquisition. He became so embarrassed by the condition of Section V that he decided to copy its contents into an entirely new ledger, a decision that set him back almost two weeks. "Elizaveta Petrovna," he wrote in one of his weekly letters, "I have begun to consider the possibility that there may be a better method for recording the contents of your collection." He did not send the letter to the Empress, but he could not forget how close he had been to sending it, and the thought brought him shame. Shuvalov had seen a man bleed for hours from a pinprick; just so, the one small fissure that had opened up in his day threatened to swallow his collection, which had become, through a steady setting aside of all other tasks, his life's work.

. . .

When Shuvalov could not concentrate on the Collection, he blamed the knocking. But there were also times when he admitted to himself that there was another distraction working on him. He had met a woman. More accurately, he had seen a woman at court, and had found that even after she passed out of his sight she did not pass out of his mind. This woman was standing underneath an archway in one of the main ballrooms, near one of the large windows that looked out over the gardens. She did not speak to Shuvalov. From what he saw, she did not speak to anyone. Her hair was as black as ink, and her dress a cream color that reminded him of parchment. She leaned against the wall and stared into the middle distance. Shuvalov was talking to Pyotor and Sergei when he first noticed the woman. He could have asked the princes if they knew her name, but he was not willing to reveal his interest. Instead, he engineered a small deceit: he wondered aloud about the architecture of the garden, and specifically about an aspect of it that he knew was foreign to both Sergei and Pyotor. "You cannot answer me?" he said, when he knew they could not. Then, feigning impatience, he walked to the window to settle the matter for himself.

On his way to the window, he turned on his heel and stared rather shamelessly at the woman. She could not have been more than twenty years old. But she had pieces of other women in her face, in the sharp angles of her nose and cheeks, in her tight, thin mouth. And her eyes were extraordinary: dark with golden flecks in them. As a younger man, Shuvalov had believed that a woman's eyes were portals to another world, but the years had divested him of this foolish notion. Now, though, he felt as though his wisdom was abandoning him.

The woman did not appear to notice Shuvalov. If she did notice him, she gave no sign. She continued to stare into the center of the ballroom, at nothing in particular. He pretended to look out the window at the garden—though in fact he looked at his own reflection, and judged himself to be still quite handsome. After waiting what he thought was an appropriate amount of time, he returned to Pyotor and Sergei. "The answer is obvious," he said, "if you would only look for yourself."

That evening, he thought of little except the woman, and the next day, when he was not worrying about the knock on the door, he was lost in his memory of her. He wondered if he would see her that afternoon, and when he did not, he wondered about the following afternoon. "Elizaveta Petrovna," he wrote in another letter he did not send to the Empress, "when a man's heart thaws, it can be a painful process, even crippling. I must confess that there are days when the Collection seems as if it might be better served by another hand, and by a clearer mind. Mine has become muddied of late, I am afraid." After wasting the better part of a week, he began a new week with a renewed sense of purpose: He was scheduled to log in a host of new works, including a Ghezzi etching of an Italian piazza, empty save for a man, boy, and a horse, and three trees that stood behind them like sentries. But he could not concentrate on it, or remember the other works to which it bore a resemblance, and instead he got up and walked to the court. The woman was nowhere to be found, and he came back to his chambers almost immediately, without thinking even once about the footsteps that he was quite sure, upon reflection, were padding along behind him. And then the knock, at two o'clock, nearly killed him, so violent was the noise, and he was able to accomplish nothing for the rest of the afternoon.

· · ·

After laboring under the influence of these distractions for three weeks, Shuvalov was so exhausted that he could hardly stay awake in the quiet of his chambers, and that, combined with his curiosity about the young woman he had seen in the ballroom, encouraged him to spend more time than usual in the court. He liked to sit on one of the green divans that was positioned in a doorway off of one of the large sitting-rooms, and to let the rest of the group arrange itself in a crescent around him. What happened in the crescent, even with an exhausted Shuvalov, was precisely what had happened before. There was Prince Pyotor haranguing another young prince about the unreadiness of the Empress's military forces. There was Prince Alexsandr, his cigar moving across the room as a rifle might. There was Prince Sergei, laughing chaotically, like something that had spilled. And yet, it was entirely different as well. Once,

Shuvalov had enjoyed the company of these men, if only because their questions and remarks helped focus him on the library; now, his suspicion fell across them like a shadow. In addition, the men seemed to go rougher with him; they had always teased him about his working habits, but now Shuvalov detected a sharp edge to their comments. "It seems to be wearing on you, this use of pen and paper," Prince Sergei said one afternoon. "I can see how that would tax a man to his limit." Then he threw back his head and brayed. Shuvalov was not listening closely to Sergei; he was looking out over his head at the crowd, trying to locate either the woman he had seen or the men who might be plaguing him by knocking at his door.

Shuvalov had ruled out some of the men as a result of their intelligence, their habits, or their temperaments. One of the men who Shuvalov knew to be innocent, Nikolai, was a tall young prince who spoke softly, with a deep voice that was a great source of pleasure for the women at court. He was a new arrival, and as a result still spent much of his time expressing admiration for the library, and hoping he might one day see the Collection. "I cannot imagine how much discipline it must take to achieve what you have achieved," he said. "You must show it to others before you present it to the Empress." Shuvalov expressed his reluctance, as he had done dozens of times before, and Nikolai grew more and more exercised, as young princes had done dozens of times before. "There is something endlessly fascinating about a record of artworks, even more fascinating than the artworks themselves," he said. "If you summarize a Hogarth print with a few brief pieces of information, such as its title, the date of its purchase, and its size, you are giving it a more honest account of its existence than a man who goes on at great length about the characters in the work, their motives and machinations. You permit another man to imagine a work of art rather than insist on one particular imagination, and that is a form of heroism."

"You speak as ardently as a student," said Shuvalov, smiling a smile he did not quite feel.

The prince laughed as if Shuvalov had been making a joke. "This is my point precisely," the prince said. "We are all students in this life. There are no teachers, only texts. We are taught by direct contact with artworks, not by the encounters between those works and other minds."

The prince went on at such length that Shuvalov's eyelids began to droop. "I must go," he said. "If not to work, then to sleep."

"Will you give me a time that I might stop by?" the Prince said.

It occurred to Shuvalov suddenly that Nikolai might be of use in helping him to identify the mystery visitor. He had been thinking of Hogarth ever since Nikolai had mentioned him, and his mind had drifted into an etching in which an older man sets a snare to catch a younger man he suspects of cuckolding him. "How about the end of next week?" Shuvalov said, low enough that no one else would hear. "At two o'clock. But if you mention the appointment to anyone, I will not honor it."

Nikolai laughed with delight. "Your secret is safe with me."

. . .

Shuvalov would have been perfectly happy to have not seen
Nikolai until he arrived at chambers at the end of the following week. The more he reflected upon the young
Prince's earnest face, the more unpleasant he found it. But a
few nights after his initial conversation, he encountered
Nikolai again. This time he had a woman on his arm. They
were coming down one of the main halls in the palace, heads
bent toward each other, and Shuvalov heard soft laughter
passing between them. "Ivan Ivanovich," the Prince called
out. Shuvalov slowed reluctantly.

It was not until they had stopped that Shuvalov recognized the woman as his woman, the young woman from the
ballroom. She was as beautiful as he remembered, and she
carried the knowledge of that beauty in her face. "Good
day," Nikolai said.

"Good day," Shuvalov said.

"Ivan Ivanovich Shuvalov. This is the Countess Natalya."

"Have we met?" Shuvalov said. He knew they had not.
But he thrilled to the faint possibility that she might say
yes. Perhaps they had met. Perhaps they were intimates
from long ago. He had a full command of all the artwork in
the Empress's possession, of all the entries in the Collection,
but he could not be counted upon to remember all that had
happened in his own life, could he? Shuvalov looked into
her eyes, and for her part the Countess did not look away.

"No," she said.

"We are on our way to a dance," Nikolai said. "But I will
see you at the end of next week." Suddenly, Shuvalov found
himself angry with the Prince.

"Yes," Shuvalov said. "In fact, I am happy to have seen you. I have something to discuss with you on that score."

"Ivan Ivanovich," Nikolai said, "I hope you are not reconsidering."

"No," Shuvalov said, "I just wonder if you would like to bring the Countess to our appointment."

Nikolai looked at Shuvalov with surprise. "But you are so reluctant to take even a single visitor."

"I think we can make an exception for the lady," he said. He turned toward the Countess and extended a hand. "I would be flattered if you would accompany the Prince to my chambers on Friday at two o'clock."

That day, Shuvalov went down the long hall remembering what he had said to the Countess, and what she had said in return. And when the two o'clock report sounded, he heard it only faintly; he had sped through the Ghezzi etching, and a Guercino canvas of the martyrdom of St. Catherine, and a painting by Cranach the Elder of two lovers in repose.

. . .

It was now the appointed day, and the clock was nearing the appointed hour, and Shuvalov was trying to enter a few more items before the Prince and the Countess arrived. He had recently purchased a plan of the city of Vienna, two pieces of Roman statuary, and a book on numismatics, and he recorded them in Collection, Section V. His favorite of the new acquisitions was a wonderful Arcimboldo, a painting on panel in which the subject's features were represented by fruits, vegetables, and flowers. The man in the picture had a nose that was a radish and ears that were ears of corn. A flower bloomed in the center of his forehead. It was a small enough work that Shuvalov had it with him in his chambers, propped up on the edge of his desk where he could look at it while he entered it into the Collection. Shuvalov felt a kinship with the portrait—he sometimes felt as if he, too, was not fully embodied, but rather built up from components, in his case the works of art he recorded in the Collection. He imagined explaining this to the Countess when she remarked on the strangeness of the Arcimboldo, which he was certain she would.

But the Arcimboldo failed where the letter to the Empress had failed before it, and before long Shuvalov was asleep. Even in his sleep, he continued to work on the Collection. But he found, to his dismay, that he was not entering works that he had acquired for the Empress. He looked around the library, or rather the library he was dreaming while he slept in his library, and found that the colors in the room were brilliant: greens and blues and yellows that leapt out at him. The reds were especially vivid, sometimes the hue of a sunset, sometimes the hue of fresh blood. Shuvalov marked them down, privately consoling himself with the knowledge that these colors were imaginary. Life was nowhere near that bold.

His eyes fluttered open, and then were drawn into sleep once more. He braced for the knock. When it came, it was tentative, delicate. He went to the door, and opened it, and was surprised to find Natalya standing on the other side of the door by herself. She had a strange expression on her face. "I was not prepared for the long walk down the hall," she said. Then she stepped forward, and as she came through the doorway her gown fell away from her, and she stood naked before him. He thought she was beautiful, and must have said something, because she returned the compliment. "You are more beautiful than I," she said. She spoke in English, a language Shuvalov did not know she possessed.

Shuvalov looked at Natalya, who was now so close to him that he could smell the scent of her body. She moved a hand over his hand; her flesh was warm and smooth, which made him fear suddenly that his was cold and rough. "These are your eyes," she said, brushing a finger across the skin beside his eyes. "This is your nose. This is your mouth." She repeated the same procedure in reverse on her own face, with his fingertips, guiding him as she went. "Now sit," she said. "And tell me all that you have seen."

He sat, her hand on his shoulder like a benediction, and recorded her entry into the room in Collection, Volume V. "Natalya," he wrote. "Appeared at door wearing gown. Came through doorway. Stood naked beside desk. Issued a statement of praise. Had a patina of perfume. Traced face and asked that face be traced."

"Turn the book to the first page." Natalya said. He had almost forgotten that she was standing there beside him, so intent was he on correctly representing what had transpired. "Turn to the first page," she repeated. He did so, and saw his own name there. "I, Shuvalov," it said. She took a step toward him. Now he could feel the heat rising off her skin. "Put your fingers on your name," she said. "Touch it." He did, and she placed her hand atop his again. Desire rushed through him; he knew that any moment now, he would see the most passionate and lurid of all reds. At the last second, she grabbed the cover of Collection, Section V and slammed the book shut on his fingers.

Shuvalov came awake with a start. He blinked his eyes to try to recapture the red, but it was gone. Natalya was gone as well. He tried to summon up a memory of her, but every image he managed to generate was composed of pieces of other portraits: eyes from Michelangelo, mouth from Titian, smooth limbs and breasts from Cranach. The clock in the corner read half past three. He tried to collect his thoughts. His heart was beating fast, and his head was pounding. No: It was not his head. It was the door. But the noise was entirely different than the noise he had been hearing each afternoon; this was a softer thudding. "Stop," Shuvalov shouted. "Please stop." He could not pull himself to his feet for a few minutes; he was still half in his dream and half in the world, and by the time he got to the door, the noise had ceased and the hallway was empty.

. . .

At court, Prince Nikolai was nowhere to be found. Shuvalov hurried to the archway where he had first seen Natalya. She was not there, of course, but the place, and the way the light came in through the window, brought her back to him. Then Shuvalov felt a presence at his back. He tensed. Could this be Natalya? A hand came to rest on his shoulder. It was a heavier hand than the hand he had dreamed. "Ivan Ivanovich," a voice said. Shuvalov turned around. It was Nikolai. "I must tell you," Nikolai said. "I came to your chambers, but you did not answer the door." Shuvalov began to apologize. "No, no," said the Prince. "I understand."

Shuvalov and the Prince looked out the window at the garden. "Do you ever feel as though you should catalog nature in addition to art?" the Prince said. "By that, I only mean to say that nature sometimes furnishes scenes that are as perfectly composed as a painting."

"I must get back to my chambers," Shuvalov said.

"Of course," said Nikolai, his tone heavy with disappointment.

Shuvalov was halfway across the ballroom when he turned back toward the Prince. "Nikolai," he said. "Would you like to accompany me to my chambers now?"

The two of them, Shuvalov in the lead, went back down the long hall toward the library. Shuvalov opened the door and the Prince stepped past him into the room. Shuvalov moved to the desk, lifted the current volume of the Collection, turned it in his hands so that the Prince could see it from every angle. Shuvalov announced that if the Prince liked, he could stay while Shuvalov worked. The Prince nodded eagerly and took a seat. Shuvalov moved into position behind his desk. He straightened the Arcimboldo so that it pleased him. He entered a French landscape that was attributed to Claude, and a Bible illustrated by Picard, and an Etruscan bust, doing his best to explain his method to the Prince, and felt his strength returning.

FRAGMENTS FROM
THE DEATH OF THE MUSICAL!
THE MUSICAL

Professor Onge's influence over the initial arrangement of this book was greater than I might have wished. I was still editing many of the stories, and even writing a few, and he not only came to the conclusion that I would furnish five of my strongest musicals and write one new one, but also managed to make that part of my official agreement with my publisher. I fulfilled the first of these terms, although a letter I received from the publisher noted that "Fragments from *Dylan! The Variety Show*" is not "technically a fake celebrity musical," and that a "variety show approximates but does not precisely satisfy the agreed-upon conditions." That letter was merely a quibble that preceded the full-blown quarrel that erupted over the sixth musical. I was, as I have said, sick of the form—sick from the top of my stovepipe hat to the soles of my worn-out shoes, to quote Abraham Lincoln—and I had decided that five celebrity musicals was enough. I was immobile on this point. I would not budge. I could no more imagine writing another musical than I could imagine drinking a gallon of vegetable oil. I sai so in a telegram, and received a telegram in return. And so we went, for months. My refusal delayed the publication of this book several times, and might be My delaying it still, were it not for the intervention of Professor Onge, who took the liberty of writing the publisher a letter introducing himself as my collaborator and suggesting a number of top-ics for this new musical. "It should be about a national/international cri-sis of some sort," he wrote, "and it should treat that crisis with a mix of light-hearted lyricism and sophisticated irony. People need singing, and never more than in a crisis."

—*B.G.*

. . .

FRAGMENTS FROM
THE DEATH OF THE MUSICAL! THE MUSICAL

{A national/international crisis happens. When this crisis occurs, a large group of people who feel that they need singing to digest their news form an organization called ALGOPWFT-TNSTDTN (A Large Group of People Who Feel That They Need Singing To Digest Their News) and immediately book a meeting room in a hotel in Salt Lake City, Utah. Then they elect a leader. His name is Bob, and he stands at the front of the room and addresses the group.}

BOB:
Colleagues, peers,
Conventioneers:
Welcome to the meeting.
Today, I fear
The hour is near.
Events are overheating.

Our hearts are filled with joy
And sadness, too, of course,
Because the planet wobbles
Like a broken-legged horse
But mostly they are joyful
Because this great snafu

Makes comedy for us

And that means comedy for you.

{BOB, who has grey hair, coughs a bit during his song. It's probably a nervous cough, not a cold, although he does have allergies. Then he cedes the floor to a woman named KATIE, who has red hair and a lovely contralto. KATIE is fairly tall—taller, in fact, than BOB, who is fairly short. KATIE has been painfully shy since childhood and always speaks with her eyes closed.}

KATIE:

Thanks, Bob.

As the leader of this group

You do a bang-up job.

You never play the fool

You never act the snob.

But Bob,

I must object.

I agree with you, except

That all the humor out there is so horrible and lame.

If I hear one more joke

From a late-night host, I'll choke.

The stupidest Jay Leno bits are garnering acclaim.

{KATIE falls. She must have been trying to step backward; instead, she twists an ankle, and boom! down she goes. Immediately, KATIE's sister, SUZETTE, springs to her feet. She has black hair.}

SUZETTE:
Excuse me, my sister, but I have a notion
About how we can mine laughter from commotion.
I know a man who can create musical, satirically
Sharp routines; his success has been proven empirically.
The man is named Ben Greenman. He lives upon a hill.
I cannot guarantee that he will help. Perhaps he will.

{Suzette, who has a cell phone, calls BEN GREENMAN, and asks him to create another musical along the lines of Elian! The Musical *or* Microsoft! The Musical, *but this one pertaining to the most recent national/international crisis. BEN GREENMAN hangs up the phone. When SUZETTE calls back, BEN GREENMAN answers the phone in a patently fake answering-machine voice and says, "BEN GREENMAN is not here right now." Then he hangs up again and turns to the mirror.}*

BEN GREENMAN:
Damn this life!
Damn it all to hell!
I have taken a solemn vow
That I would bid farewell
To this entire genre: No more current events.
The failure of imagination that it represents
Ashames me.
So don't blame me
If I flatly refuse.
I'd rather be gang-raped by kangaroos.

{Back in Salt Lake City, BOB bandages KATIE's foot. While

he is bandaging her foot, his hand brushes her thigh. They fall in love. BOB sings a stirring ballad, "I Bandaged Her Foot (And She Bandaged My Heart)" which will not, for reasons of space, be reprinted here. Then KATIE informs BOB, SUZETTE, and the assembled group that she has a friend named Lorena who is a beauty queen. "Actually," KATIE says, "she won the contest, but they was stripped of her crown for sleeping with the judges. I say that we send her to tempt BEN GREENMAN, and to trick him into writing another current-events musical." KATIE finishes speaking and opens her eyes to find BOB and SUZETTE smiling at her. "Do you want to call Lorena on my cell phone?" SUZETTE says. KATIE nods. LORENA picks up on the first ring.}

LORENA:
I'll happily do it.
I'll do it without pause.
I'll do it for
This very worthy cause.

{BOB, KATIE, and SUZETTE go to the hotel pool, and wait while Lorena carries out her mission. LORENA goes to visit BEN GREENMAN at his house on top of the hill. It is a huge house, with a huge front door. When he opens the door, she gasps: He is a shriveled old man with wild greasy hair. Still, he is polite, and invites her inside. Once she is inside, he removes his Shriveled Old Man costume, revealing himself to be a young man, albeit still with greasy hair.}

BEN GREENMAN:
I know why you have come up here.
I just simply won't do it.

The prospect of a musical
Makes me want to vomit.

I've done them all: the Cuban boy,
The model, the tycoon.
The future of this nation
Cannot be set to music.

*{LORENA smiles mysteriously. She and BEN GREENMAN
disappear behind closed doors. Birds sing and strings swell to
metaphorically indicate intercourse. Eight minutes later, BEN
GREENMAN emerges from behind the closed door.}*

BEN GREENMAN:
I'm sorry to say
That I woke up today
With a song in my heart
That soon spread to my head.
I thought I had disposed
Of all these songs.
I was wrong
I suppose

*{BEN GREENMAN saddles up his kangaroos, looks long-
ingly into their liquid brown eyes, then unsaddles them, saddles up
his horses, and rides down to Salt Lake City. When he arrives,
BOB comes out of the pool and towels off. KATIE and SUZETTE
stay in the pool. "We don't mean to be rude," SUZETTE says.
"But the water is the perfect temperature." KATIE nods. "It helps
my foot," she says. BOB runs a hand through his hair and then*

extends that same hand to BEN GREENMAN. "Nice to meet you," he says. "We've heard so much about you." BEN GREENMAN nods. "I assume," BOB says, "that LORENA has made our interest in your talents quite evident." BEN GREENMAN nods again. "You see," BOB says, "with the recent national/international crisis and all, we're looking for a way to turn it into intelligent, probing comedy, and we heard that you are our man." BOB is the kind of guy who will explain something even if he's just been told that it needs no explanation. "I think I can safely speak for KATIE and SUZETTE when I say that we are all great admirers of your work." BOB then bends down and retrieves a notebook. "This morning," he says, "after we sent LORENA off to meet you, I jotted down some ideas of things I personally found funny, little wrinkles in this latest national/international crisis that are, if not absurd, at least mildly humorous." KATIE, who by now no longer loves BOB, takes a deep breath and begins to swim the length of the pool. SUZETTE stands in the shallow end and thinks ahead to dinner. BEN GREENMAN sits down on a lounge chair. He takes off his shoes. He has a feeling he's going to be there all day. But no sooner does BEN GREENMAN sit down than he sees that BOB has a gun. How did this escape his notice? BOB fires a number of shots in the air. Some birds fall down around the pool. Then BOB turns back toward BEN GREENMAN. "I know what you're thinking," BOB says. "Did he fire five shots or six? Well, to tell you the truth, in all this commotion I've lost track myself. So you got to ask yourself one question. Do you feel lucky? Well, do you, punk?" BEN GREENMAN counts the birds: one, two, three, four. Next to the fourth is a white form he cannot identify. Is it a bird or a hand towel? BEN GREENMAN smiles at BOB. BOB scowls at BEN

GREENMAN. *The trigger comes down tentatively, as if it doesn't know the answer either.*}

MARLON BRANDO'S DREAMING

To the door of my modest country home in the placid British town of S., there arrived a package—a nondescript box of the sort favored by online retailers, department stores, catalog houses, shops that line the main streets of S., and, in short, all business who concern themselves with the sale and delivery of goods. In the box was scattered a load of styrofoam peanuts—or rather, I thought that they were styrofoam, and did not consider until later the possibility that they might have been those starch packing peanuts that dissolve in water and can therefore be eaten in large quantities as a means of shocking friends and acquaintances. Larry King, for example. In addition, there was a blue bottle that, while not large, was not small either. Also, while not ornate, it was not plain. It had no label, even when I turned it around. I searched through the foam peanuts for a card or a packing slip, but found none. I called my lady friend, whose name eluded me at that moment, to see if she could find any information as to the package's origin, but she was not around. She had, since earlier in the day, been outside with the gardener, huddled in counsel over the fate of the peonies. Then I grew bored, and placing the bottle on top of the dresser by the front door, went upstairs to the bedroom, where I fell into a deep sleep that took the shape of a dream of intensely aerobic carnal congress with a certain starlet of the forties whose films, I am sorry to say, were far inferior to her physical charms.

During the night the bottle fell but did not break. My lady friend—by then I had remembered her name, which was Taluwa—did not join me in my bedroom, but rather slept in her own, and my sleep was rich and rewarding. Coming down for my customary breakfast of eggs and loaves of bread, I noticed it on the floor by the stairs, where it had rolled after its plunge from the dresser. I called for Taluwa again, and this time she answered, but only to tell me that she was still working with the gardener, not on the peonies any longer but on the particularly knotty problem of a potted palm. To my ears, her voice carried, in addition to its usual seductive cast, a tinge of impatience. Ever since I brought her here from the island of Ponape in the Eastern Caroline Islands, she has often been short-tempered with me, sometimes inappropriately. I took a nap during breakfast, and another one just after breakfast, and then I picked the bottle up and placed it back on the dresser.

When I awoke from my after-breakfast nap, it was because the gardener, a little man who favored large sweaters, had entered the house. I thought he was Jewish, although I had never known a Jewish gardener. I thought this only because when I asked him if he would like to join me in a brandy, he declined. Jews aren't big drinkers.

Also, once about six months previous, I was typing up a letter to *The New York Times* that discussed the wonderful tendency of the Jew to engage in spirited verbal banter, and the gardener wandered by my desk and fixed me with a look of what I took to be silent disapproval, I assumed ironically. That day, the gardener picked up the bottle, then disappeared upstairs to Taluwa's bedroom to collect something. When he emerged again, he had in his hands what he wished me to think was the same bottle, but what I saw upon closer inspection was an entirely different bottle, narrower at the top, wider at the bottom, and of a hue that tended more toward periwinkle than toward cobalt. As soon as he was outside, I smashed this impostor-bottle into a thousand pieces, then ate some old lasagna I found hiding in the back of the refrigerator. The sauce, once red, had turned a brownish color that I can only describe as "brown-red." If there is a more precise term for this hue, I must confess that I do not know it.

My intent after eating the lasagna was to march right into Taluwa's bedroom and look for the original bottle, after which I would replace it on the dresser where it belonged. But while I was still wiping the last drabs of tomato sauce from my neck, I suffered a dizzy spell that swiftly did away with any thought of ascending the stairs. My episodes, as Taluwa likes to call them, began about ten years ago as infrequent nuisances. Today, they are so common that I cannot often distinguish them from their absence. When they come upon me, my mind melts into a muddle. In *The Island of Dr. Moreau*, a film I consider to be my greatest accomplishment, I wrote much of my own dialogue, including the film's greatest line of dialogue, which also happens to be the greatest line of dialogue ever spoken in the history of cinema: "I have seen the devil in my microscope, and I have chained him." When Val Kilmer heard me speak that line for the first time, he fell to his knees. David Thewlis told me later that he thought that Val had simply tripped over one of the man-beast costumes, but I refuse to listen to jealous chatter. Were I to remake that film, and it is entirely possible that I might, I would rewrite the greatest line of dialogue ever spoken in the history of cinema to make it even greater. "I have seen the devil in my mind," I would say, "and I have claimed him." Let Thewlis tell me that any man who falls to his knees in the wake of that line is merely tripping over a half-lion's-head, half-man's-head mask!

But my dizzy spell has distracted the course of my tale. After dashing the blue bottle to pieces, I thought that I was done with the saga of the mysterious vessel. I could not have been more wrong. When I broke it, I noticed a slight smell of sulfur, but did not think anything of it. But when I was eating the wienerschnitzel, which followed the lasagna, I was overpowered by another smell, that of roses. I thought for certain that the scent was somehow connected to the gardener, but neither he nor Taluwa were anywhere to be found. And when I undertook to locate the source of the perfume, I traced it to the spatter of blue glass. I stood over the remnants of the bottle, and then it came to me: the contents of the bottle, first sulfurous and then with the aroma of roses, were the contents of my soul, which had been regrettably demonic when I was a young ruffian but had blossomed into floral enlightenment late in life. Before my eyes, as if responding to my spark of inner vision, the pieces began to reassemble themselves into a whole bottle, and not just any bottle but the very same bottle that I had received in the mail, the very same bottle that the Jewish gardener had spirited upstairs. I quaked with fear. My knees clapped against one another. I almost dropped the fudgsicle that I clutched with my right hand.

I have not always been receptive to the supernatural. When I first arrived in New York City to study acting, I was, as I have said, willful and reckless, and hardly heeded the laws of man, let alone those of the heavens. But with age, I have learned to read my surroundings for traces of the divine—not just tea leaves and crop circles, but less well-known sources of augury, like the bottom of a rapidly ingested gallon tub of vanilla ice cream. This particular tub, to which I fled after the bottle's resurrection, had a faint yellow streak that brought to mind butter, which in turn brought to mind joy. Suddenly, I felt a stabbing pain in the lower left quadrant of my belly. I palpated there but could find nothing. It seared for a few excruciating seconds, then went as quickly as it had come, leaving behind a newly minted relief. I walked into the living room, where the wicker rocker in the corner beckoned me. I fell into its embrace, and then into the outstretched arms of sleep. The starlet who had visited my dream the night before was there again, this time sitting by herself on a red sofa, investigating herself in a manner that has not been shown on the silver screen since the days before the Hays Code. Flushing with embarrassment and pleasure both, feeling my age, I knelt at her feet, knees creaking loudly, and prayed for her to save me.

FUN WITH TIME

Obtain a watch without fluorescent-tipped hands. Go into a pitch-black room. Hold the watch to your ear. Then close your eyes. Is the ticking any louder?

Locate a small child who can speak but not yet tell time. Ask the child what time it is. When the child answers, believe him.

Find an ordinary kitchen timer and set it for three minutes. At the conclusion of the three minutes, divorce your wife or husband. If you are not married, marry the first available person, reset the timer, and repeat the exercise.

Each time the minute hand overlaps the hour hand, pretend that the hour hand has disappeared. As quickly as possible, work yourself into a panic imagining a world with no hours, only minutes.

The next time you feel happy, look at a clock and note how

long it takes until you are miserable.

When a friend asks you what time it is, say, "Time to take off my watch and put it in my pocket." Then take off your watch and put it in your pocket.

WHAT 100 PEOPLE, REAL AND FAKE, BELIEVE ABOUT DOLORES

Ruth, her friend: That she never meant to hurt Tom.

Arthur, Tom's brother: That if she never meant to hurt Tom, then she probably wouldn't have done the things that she did.

Max, Tom's friend: That she was young and immature and that she was on the outs with Tom almost from the minute they started dating.

Hal, Tom's friend: That she was almost as tall as Tom.

Anne, her mother: That she was a young woman who always wanted certain things from life. That a husband was one of them. That when she said a husband, she meant someone wealthy, not a millionaire necessarily, but someone with a stable job. That she wanted someone who wasn't her father.

Lou, her father: That she was a beautiful girl, and that he

was sorry that he left when he did, and that over the last twenty years he thought about her often.

Sigmund Freud: That she had issues with her father's abandonment, and that it was a major contributor to her romantic pattern.

Superman: That the underwear she wore was the same as the underwear that Lois Lane wore.

Heather, her childhood friend: That she was beautiful when she was young.

June, her college roommate: That she was beautiful when she was young.

Gina, her college roommate: That she thought she was beautiful, and that she worried about it all the time.

Paul, her former boyfriend: That she was beautiful when she didn't worry too much about being beautiful. That she was different from her mother and her sister, darker, a little more dangerous.

Modigliani: That she was a woman he might have painted, and did, many times.

Don Quixote: That she was a beautiful princess, almost as beautiful as Dulcinea.

Keith, her college friend: That she liked to say that she was imprisoned in a man's body, with a man's mind and a man's eye.

Frank, her college friend: That when she joked about being a gay man, she wasn't joking entirely. That when they met, they were both sophomores, and he was out, very out, flamboyantly so, and she came right up to him after class and said, "I know all about you," and he said, "I'm sorry," very archly, and she said, "I know all about you because I am just like you." That they were friends from then on.

Leila, her younger sister: That she spent too much time on the telephone, and was bossy, but that when she went away to college the house was too quiet.

Nancy, her former boss: That she worked in an ice-cream shop during high school as a scooper, and that there was some money missing from the register during her shift. That when she was confronted, she swore that she had nothing to do with it and didn't know a thing about it. That she seemed too nervous and defiant for someone who didn't know a thing about it.

Dick Tracy: That she did not do her part in fighting crime.

Kim, her college friend: That she didn't know what she wanted to do after graduation. That she stumbled into politics because that's what Kevin was doing.

Isabel, her college friend: That Kevin was her first great love.

Kevin, her former boyfriend: That she didn't have an easy time with things, that she would cry sometimes for no good reason, that she ground her teeth when she slept. That she was ashamed of this sadness, and furious that it appeared sometimes in the office, or in the car. That once, when he caught her crying in the shower and reached out to touch her shoulder, she blinked her sorrow away, just closed her eyes and when she opened them was disconcertingly serene. That she said, "What," and though he had come to console her he found himself suddenly overmastered. That it was as if he were the patient and she the doctor. That he felt a bit humiliated, and murmured an apology, and slunk out of the bathroom. That she emerged later to continue her interrogation, and asked if he considered her an object of pity. That he said of course not. That she scowled, and then smirked. That when she left three weeks later, and it came as a complete surprise, he should have known what she meant when she said that men were always more blind than women.

George, her former boyfriend: That she said she had never loved Kevin. That she said that she had never been in love at all. That she said that it was about sex, mostly, and friendship, a little bit. That she wanted to stay in politics but wanted to work for a different campaign. That introducing her to Jim was a mistake, because Jim introduced her to Tom.

Jim, her co-worker: That she was the right woman for the job. That the campaign needed a good press assistant, someone who was personable and pretty but could also smell blood and go in for the kill. That she was a great friend, for a while.

Maurice, her co-worker: That she brightened up the place.

Demetria, her co-worker: That she was fun in elevators. That it's a strange thing to remember, but very vivid: Once in an elevator, she pretended that the car had stopped between floors and made up an elaborate story about what would happen, the rescue, the injuries. That this was apparently not the only time she had done this.

Hannah, her co-worker: That it was love at first sight for her and Tom. That you could almost see a little arc of electricity between them. That if Tom hadn't been Jim's cousin, she would have run off with him right then and there. That she restrained herself out of friendship for Tom, although it's not anything she would admit. That when she found out that Jim and Tom didn't get along all that well, she called Tom herself and asked him out to dinner.

Captain Ahab: That he would have liked to meet her.

Wendy, Tom's mother: That she was good for Tom. That she was tough, but Tom needed some toughening up, since if he was left to his own devices he would have just kept on with his novel, or his play, or whatever it was he was writing that day.

Bruce, Tom's father: That she reminded him of his wife.

Seth, Tom's younger brother: That she was cool. That after she and Tom moved in together, she used to have great parties and invite all the younger kids and not make a big deal about drinking or anything. That she was hot, too.

Howard Atkin, waiter: That she and Tom tipped well.

Oscar Johnson: That she wasn't one of those people who looked at you funny if you were down on your luck. That she gave money to you if you asked for it.

Randy, Tom's friend: That she wasn't so helpful. That when she and Tom got the apartment, a bunch of friends went over to give them a hand. That she said she was supervising.

Tom Sawyer: That she would not have painted the fence.

Jennifer Antone, psychologist: That she and Tom moved in together too quickly. That she had unresolved parts of her personality that were clearly not going to resolve without some hard work. That she was uncertain about her career choice, and a little resentful that so much of the work fell to her with so little of the credit. That she had discovered something about the Senator.

Frida, her friend: That she had discovered something about the Senator, or that at the very least her attitude toward him changed. That he had been a kind of father figure to her at first, but that after a while he was someone she didn't quite trust.

Leo, her co-worker: That she started to put in longer hours after the first six months. That usually she wasn't the only one there late. That Demetria or Jim would stay, too. That she would call Tom and tell him that she wouldn't be home until late. That she would say, "Don't wait up," like it was a line she heard from a movie.

Senator Charles Gowdy: That she was an excellent employee, both during the campaign and after the election, never late to work, never in a bad mood, always curious, always pleasant.

Sammy Glick: That she was kissing ass to get ahead.

Janice, her grandmother: That an old woman shouldn't say bad things about a young woman, and a grandmother especially shouldn't say bad things about her granddaughter, but that there was something off about her. That maybe it's not so bad to criticize if what you're criticizing is something you recognize in yourself. That there was a woman once who worked for Senator Lyndon Johnson some forty years earlier, and that this woman had a dalliance with Senator Johnson that lasted a few months and took place mostly in hotels and limousines. That this woman had no regrets, and that her granddaughter was cut from the same cloth. That the young woman liked for a time to pretend that the Senator had disappointed her as a way of putting distance between the two of them, but that the spark in her eyes gave her away.

Lyndon B. Johnson: That if that girl didn't fuck that

Senator, politics ain't what it used to be.

Doris, Tom's grandmother: That she had a man who loved her, and that she made him sad. That it would have been nosy to ask more. That Tom came down to Florida and moped like he was still fourteen years old and sweet on his first crush.

Ralph Kramden: That she should have been sent to the moon.

Luciana, her friend: That she and Tom hit a bump and that it made her really angry. That she said that he should have trusted her instead of running away. That she said that things would work out, one way or another, with or without Tom. That she laughed when she said it like she didn't quite believe it.

Cindy, Tom's friend: That she might have been fooling around with a girl, or at least Tom thought so.

Arthur Morris, bus driver: That she wore a skirt one time that was cut up the side so high that you could see right clear to her parts.

T-2: That she knew that violence was no solution.

Julie, her neighbor: That when she moved into the apartment building, she and Tom were going through a rough patch. That he had accused her of seeing someone else behind his back, and she had admitted it, and they were separating for a few months to see how things felt. That she was upset enough by this to talk about it to a total stranger in the elevator on her first day in the building.

Warren, her neighbor: That she worked terribly late hours. That she traveled on weekends, sometimes with the Senator. That after about six months in that new building, she moved out. That she had reconciled with her boyfriend and was moving back in with him. That she was going to cut back her work hours and try to live a more normal life. That that's what she said, "more normal life." That she was excited enough about this to talk about it to a total stranger late at night in the lobby of the building.

Pauline, her friend: That although she thought that Tom would take her back with no conditions, he was pretty angry and had in fact already moved on a little bit, that he had been with other women and thought about life without her, and that the things he wanted from her were at that point demanded rather than asked.

Peter, her second cousin: That he hadn't seen her since she was a little kid, when her father used to take her around from bar to bar. That she sat down on a stool and ordered a beer and then announced who she was. That she looked terrible, not just exhausted but distracted, and that she said that she had just moved back in with her boyfriend, which was good, but that he had kicked her out for the night, which was bad.

Pvt. Carl Radizio: That when he met her in a bar down-town, she was drunk, because that's the only reason she would have called him "Honey" from the start. Also, that she was still drunk later that night, when she went home with him and told him that she had always had a fantasy about soldiers.

Uncle Sam: That she was good for morale.

Andy Warhol: That she could have been even more fantastic.

Trisha, her childhood friend: That she would become a famous singer, because that's what she always said she want-ed to be.

Jack, high school music teacher: That she was extraordinar-ily gifted.

Paul, college music teacher: That she had been told, some-where along the way, that she was extraordinarily gifted, and that it got in the way of actual development of her tal-ent, which was considerable.

Billie Holiday: That she could get inside a song and live there.

Lorraine, her friend: That she had some trouble being faith-ful. That she was seeing this guy Jay at the same time that she was seeing Kevin, and that she said that they wouldn't find out because she was so different with the two of them that they probably thought they were seeing different girls. That she was sad with Kevin and kept herself feeling small. That she was happy with Jay, and sang all the time.

Jay, her former boyfriend: That she had a beautiful voice. That she used to sing in the shower, amazing old jazz songs. That she said that she would rather sing in the shower than have sex in the shower, but that she did both.

Gervaise, her friend: That she said she wasn't planning on voting for the Senator when he came up for re-election. That she laughed and said that she hadn't voted for him the first time. That she laughed again and said that she had never voted at all.

Elizabeth Cady Stanton: That she squandered her hard-fought right to vote.

Paolo, Tom's friend: That she was bad for him, because when they were apart, he suddenly started to produce work. That in three years with her, he had managed to write only a handful of stories, but that without her he wrote hundreds of pages in three months. That it was much better than the things he had written with her.

Martine, former college professor: That she had trouble growing up. That it was easy to keep an eye on her, since she was usually the one who filled up a room. That she went from high school to college on this wave of achievement and ambition, and that she hit a kind of wall where boys became as important to her as anything else. That after college, she wrote letters, and those letters were mostly about small rips and tears in her identity, until she met Tom, and then the letters were about being happy, which was for her a rarity.

Dracula: That she had a lovely neck.

Virginia Andrews, psychologist: That she was conflicted about her sexual identity, which is not particularly surprising, since most people are to some degree, but that she was unusually articulate about it. That she was not faithful to Tom and had not been faithful to Tom since the beginning of their relationship, that in fact she saw her time with Tom was itself a kind of infidelity to a previous boyfriend, and so on and so on. That she viewed herself as a gay man, and said so several times, and drew parallels between herself and her gay male friends, such as a certain promiscuity, a certain secrecy, a certain defensiveness. That her relationship with her father was almost certainly at the root of these problems.

Margaret Brel, psychologist: That she switched therapists when they told her things she didn't want to hear, which is a dangerous practice. That she had been seeing Jennifer Antone, who is a wonderful psychologist, until Jennifer told her that she needed to deal with her feelings about her father. That she moved on to Ginny Andrews, and that didn't seem to work out, and she left for Don Rogers, who is not much of an analyst but has a wonderfully comforting manner, and that evidently even Don was too confrontational for her. That she used to fight Don on even the simplest recommendation. That Don eventually said, "Why don't you go see Dr. Brel?"

Don Rogers, psychologist: That she was extremely seductive. That patients had been seductive before, sometimes even attractive female patients, but that she had a certain determination that made it problematic to keep her as a patient.

Mary Poppins: That she was always complicating things that were really quite simple.

Elisabeth, Tom's sister: That she and Tom both seemed frustrated after they moved back in with each other.

Janice, Tom's former girlfriend: That she was friendly enough, even though she knew that Tom hadn't exactly been by himself during the time they were separated. That she said that she wanted to be very clear about her relationship with him.

Elaine, Tom's friend: That she was genuinely happy when Tom found a publisher for his book.

Trudy, co-worker: That she wanted to leave the Senator's office. That she wasn't hiding it, so much, because that was one of the first things she said when you met her. That her boyfriend had just sold a book, and that his agent thought it might be a great screenplay.

Patrice, neighbor: That she and Tom were the guests of

honor at a party that a friend was giving for Tom. That she was nervous about it because she hadn't seen lots of his friends since before the first time they broke up.

Jackie, Tom's friend: That she was so thankful that she didn't have to have the party at her house. That she said she was a horrible hostess. That she helped plan, though, and helped make the food. That she felt like things were looking up for her and Tom, and that the time apart had been a great help.

Doug, party guest: That she drank too much too early and started talking about how she hadn't really ever known her father.

Marcus, Tom's agent: That she got completely drunk and went around telling everyone that Tom's book was about her. That Tom's book was in fact about a young athlete, a runner, who ripped up his right leg in a car accident and then embarked on a career as an artist. That when someone asked her about this she admitted that she hadn't read Tom's book and wandered off to get another drink.

Ariana, party guest: That she got completely drunk and started hitting on everyone there. That it didn't matter if they were men and women. That she kissed a woman out on the patio.

Jane, party guest: That they had a fight, she and Tom.

Kimberly, party guest: That they had a fight, she and Tom.

Robin Hood: That they had a fight, she and Tom.

Calvin Coolidge: That they had a fight, she and Tom.

Paula, party guest: That they had a fight, she and Tom, and that by the end she was screaming.

Luke Skywalker: That she left the party without Tom.

Yolanda, neighbor: That she came home from the party without Tom.

Marcel Duchamp: That she turned on the television and sunk into a chair.

Mariel Hemingway: That she poured herself a drink, and then poured herself another drink.

Aristotle: That she expected that Tom would come through the door at one, or two, but that he didn't.

Marvin Gaye: That she expected that Tom would come through the door at three, or four, but he didn't.

Betsy Ross: That she expected that Tom would at least call her, but he didn't.

Paul McCartney: That she kept watching television.

Jay Gatsby: That she turned on both televisions, the one in

the bedroom and the one in the living room.

Popeye: That she sat between them. That the blue glow of the TV sets sank into her until it became indistinguishable from her very being.

Lucy Ricardo: That if you're on television every night, you're poured into so many homes that you can hardly keep track of them. That now and again you pick up a signal from one place or another, and you pay closer attention. That if a baby is being born in a house with the set on, you can sense that. That you can also sense suicides. That one night, during the episode with the blacked-out teeth, she started staring straight ahead. That her eyes were open, but that she didn't laugh or cry or anything, just stared. That it was as if she was gone out of her body. That she was like that for more than twenty minutes. That when she finally got up to change the channel it was a relief, because whatever happened to her after that couldn't have been good.

Tracy, Tom's friend: That Tom came over and slept on the floor. That Tom was drunk and Tom was angry. That Tom said it was over between the two of them.

Lt. Oswaldo Sepulveda: That she placed a call to the precinct saying that someone had tampered with the locks on her front door.

Lt. Columbo: That there was something suspicious about the way that Tom's car was parked outside Tracy's apartment. That there was also something suspicious about the fact that there were no signs of tampering on the front door lock. That there was something suspicious about the fact that her phone was off the hook, and that his car battery was dead.

Tom: That he never meant to hurt her.